THE VIRGIN REPLAY

LAUREN BLAKELY

LAUREN BLAKELY BOOKS

Cover Design by Helen Williams.

ALSO BY LAUREN BLAKELY

Big Rock Series

Big Rock

Mister O

Well Hung

Full Package

Joy Ride

Hard Wood

Rules of Love Series

The Rules of Friends with Benefits (A Prequel Novella)

The Virgin Rule Book

The Virgin Game Plan

The Virgin Replay

The Viring Scorecard

Men of Summer Series

Scoring With Him

Winning With Him

All In With Him

The Guys Who Got Away Series

Dear Sexy Ex-Boyfriend

The What If Guy

Thanks for Last Night

The Dream Guy Next Door

The Gift Series

The Engagement Gift

The Virgin Gift

The Decadent Gift

The Extravagant Series

One Night Only

One Exquisite Touch

My One-Week Husband

MM Standalone Novels

A Guy Walks Into My Bar

One Time Only

The Bromance Zone

The Heartbreakers Series

Once Upon a Real Good Time

Once Upon a Sure Thing

Once Upon a Wild Fling

Boyfriend Material

Asking For a Friend

Sex and Other Shiny Objects

One Night Stand-In

Lucky In Love Series

Best Laid Plans

The Feel Good Factor

Nobody Does It Better

Unzipped

Always Satisfied Series

Satisfaction Guaranteed

Instant Gratification

Overnight Service

Never Have I Ever

PS It's Always Been You

Special Delivery

The Sexy Suit Series

Lucky Suit

Birthday Suit

From Paris With Love

Wanderlust

Part-Time Lover

One Love Series

The Sexy One

The Only One

The Hot One

The Knocked Up Plan

Come As You Are

Sports Romance

Most Valuable Playboy

Most Likely to Score

Standalones

Stud Finder

The V Card

The Real Deal

Unbreak My Heart

The Break-Up Album

The Caught Up in Love Series

The Pretending Plot (previously called *Pretending He's Mine*)

The Dating Proposal

The Second Chance Plan (previously called *Caught Up In Us*)

The Private Rehearsal (previously called *Playing With Her Heart*)

Seductive Nights Series

Night After Night

After This Night

One More Night

A Wildly Seductive Night

ABOUT

A virgin, an athlete, a fake romance, and only one bed in the hotel room.

Following rules shot me to the top of my game as an all-star baseball player, and the golden rule is this—don't hookup with your teammate's sister.

But ask her to be your fake date when you desperately need one for a family wedding?

Nothing in the guy code against that. Plus, the flirty, feisty Sierra's my friend too, so why the hell not pretend we're madly in lust for two days in Hawaii? No hardship in a make believe kiss here, a fake smooch there, as long as we don't cross any dangerous lines.

Then, the hotel books us into the same suite. Which means she's showering near me, putting on itty bitty bikinis in the same room, sliding into that king-size bed wearing only a black lace cami.

But I resist…until the night she tells me she's been waiting for me to be her first.

And there's nothing fake about my desire to say yes, even though that's definitely against the code. But, maybe only if someone catches feelings?
And neither one of us will.
Until I do...

THE VIRGIN REPLAY

By Lauren Blakely

Want to be the first to learn of sales, new releases, preorders and special freebies? Sign up for my VIP mailing list here!

HER PROLOGUE

Some women collect postcards from their travels. Some collect colorful apothecary jars.

Me? I have a thing for . . . pretty little things.

Scraps of lace.

Bits of satin.

Snippets of silk.

I don't even believe in saving them for dates, or for men, or for, *gasp*, sex.

I wear sexy matching lingerie every damn day of the week.

Red, black, pink. Striped, polka dotted, floral. Bring on the hip-hugging, breast-boosting secret luxuries.

They make me feel so many things—mostly like a badass babe in charge of my own destiny.

That's not something I had when I was younger, but I've craved it over the years. I've sought out control in nearly every aspect of my life. Control over my choices, control over romance, and I suppose, control over men.

I don't mean dominatrix-style control.

All I mean is that I'm *picky*. I don't trust easily. Trust is hard won, and when it comes to romance, I haven't experienced it at all.

Trouble is, I'd very much like to have the other things that come with romance. The red-hot tangles in the sheets. The wild, sexy nights.

And I'd like to have them with a certain someone.

Admittedly, I've been weighing the option of *this guy* for the last year.

As in, every time a certain tall, dark, handsome, and charming man walks into my bar, I imagine his face if he undressed me and glimpsed what I wore next to my skin.

Which tells me . . . it's finally time for this badass babe to make a daring proposition.

HIS PROLOGUE

Two things I always knew I wanted to be when I grew up—a ballplayer and a guy my teammates could rely on.

Baseball is hard, but the rules are straightforward: throw the ball, hit the ball, catch the ball.

It helps to have a ninety-eight-mile-an-hour fastball and wicked control. It's a bonus that I play well with others. That's how I've become one of the top closers in the Major Leagues.

As long as you follow the rules, being a good teammate off the field doesn't have to be complicated either.

One: don't run off at the mouth like a dipshit. Especially not in front of reporters, fans, the public, or anyone with a cell phone camera. Which is everyone these days.

Two: don't be a dick, and don't *show* your dick online.

Three: don't post pictures of yourself skunk-faced trashed, and maybe don't get so trashed that it seems like a good idea in the first place.

Finally, don't hook up within two degrees of separation from a teammate.

No moms, daughters, or sisters.

Fortunately, I've had zero temptation and zero trouble. My mouth doesn't lead me into trouble, and my dick hasn't either, since I was married and faithful for ten years.

But thanks to one helluva vicious heartbreak and a brutal divorce, I've been single for 365 days and 365 nights of solitude.

Lately, though, I wouldn't mind the company of one woman in particular. A woman who's fierce, stunning, and fantastically sarcastic.

I'd like to take her out.

Take her home.

Indulge in a few hot dates of the all-night-long variety.

But I don't slide into Sierra's DMs with a hookup request. Why?

Because the woman I want isn't merely the bar owner around the corner.

She's a teammate's sister.

And good guys don't ask a teammate's sister for hot, sweaty, forget-the-world sex.

Until I discover a way to bend this guideline. *With her.*

Maybe I'm a good guy with a secret bad boy streak.

1

SIERRA

I'm pretty good at reading people—comes with being a bartender. But there's one customer I haven't been able to get a read on in the last year.

The guy who's putting the pool cues away in the game room at my bar.

At least, I can't get a read as to whether he'll ever ask me out.

Or ask me to go home with him.

With everyone else gone for the night and The Spotted Zebra already closed, I steal a moment to check out Chance Ashford as he lifts his multimillion-dollar right arm to place the sticks in the holder on the wall.

I'm enjoying the view of him *a lot*. Every time he comes by, I enjoy the view a little more. And then I wonder . . .

When he's done, the tall drink of a man turns around, wipes one palm across the other, and flashes me a winning grin. "That's done."

Best to keep things friendly, as they've always been,

till I know where we might go from here. “Watch out. I just might enlist you in mopping and cleaning up,” I say breezily.

His chocolate-brown eyes twinkle. “I just might say yes.”

I laugh, then hook my thumb in the direction of the door. “Hit the road, Chance. You’ve got playoffs to rest up for.”

Chance is the closing pitcher for the San Francisco Cougars, my second-favorite baseball team in the city. Since my brother became their starting catcher, the team has grown on me. Some of the guys on the team have become close friends over the last few years, stopping by my bar after games.

Like this man.

Chance is obviously far and away my favorite of the guys who stop by. He’s easy to talk to and so damn easy on the eyes.

“I don’t mind helping. Our first playoff game isn’t for a couple days, so I don’t have an early bedtime tonight. Besides, I’m still amped up from clinching.”

I reach for a couple shot glasses left on the pool table. “But it’s late, and star closers need their beauty sleep.”

“That is true. Sleep is a beautiful thing. But I’ll still help you finish up.”

I can do it myself, but the team stayed late. The crowd was boisterous, and I won’t turn down an extra pair of hands at this post-midnight hour.

And *those hands . . .*

As he gathers the beer bottles from the pool table, I

study his long strong fingers and big palms that can wrap around a baseball. And perhaps a woman's hips.

Mmm, I like that image.

And what are you going to do about it, Sierra?

"Take these to the kitchen?"

I blink. Look up. Meet his eyes. A flush crawls up my chest as it takes me a few seconds to process his question.

"Yes, thanks," I say, my throat a little dry.

Good thing he didn't entirely catch me staring.

Chance takes the empties to the kitchen, places the bottles in the recycling, then sets the glasses in the sink. As we make quick work of washing and drying, I do my best to reroute my thoughts.

I can't keep crushing on him like this.

Or is it lusting?

Probably a little of both.

Chance finishes setting the chairs on the tables, and I decide that tonight, it's a crush. When I'm ready to say goodnight to The Spotted Zebra, I grab my purse from behind the counter and head for the door.

He holds it open for me.

"Thanks again. I appreciate it. You didn't have to stay behind," I say as I lock up the bar.

"I know I didn't have to. I wanted to," he says, his sexy voice a delicious rumble.

The crushy, lusty feeling definitely includes affection too. How can I help it when Chance looks at me with such genuine kindness, like it truly was his pleasure to help me out?

Kindness in a man I lust after? That would be potent.

He glances at his wrist even though he doesn't wear a watch. "It's late. Are you calling a Lyft or walking?"

I gesture in the direction of my apartment a few blocks away. "I don't live far. I'll walk."

He gives a crisp nod. "Then I'll walk you. And don't say I don't have to."

With a laugh, I gesture to the sidewalk. "I won't say that."

As we head down the block, we pass a group of fans decked out in Cougars gear, still a little rowdy from the team's victory, which secured them a Wild Card spot. A guy in glasses recognizes Chance, thrusts an arm in the air, and shouts, "Go, Cougs."

"Go, Cougs," Chance replies.

"So, I'm a little torn on something," I say once we turn on the next block.

"Yeah? What's that?"

"Who to root for in the playoffs."

He strokes his bearded jaw as if he's deep in thought. "Oh. Of course. That sounds like such a difficult dilemma."

I shrug. "It's not so easy. I've always been a Dragons woman."

He staggers, clasping a hand over his heart. "You did not just say that."

"I did," I say cheekily as we walk on. "More to the point, haven't you noticed my brother and I love to bicker about team versus family loyalty?"

Chance shakes his head in disbelief. "Grant is my

catcher. How can you *not* be a Cougars fan? I assumed you were simply giving your sibling some sass."

"You know what they say about making assumptions," I tease.

He shakes a finger at me. "That's a reasonable expectation, woman."

"Maybe it is. But one should always ask."

"Fine. You have me there. So, I'll ask now—why are you breaking my heart, Sierra?"

"I grew up a Dragons fan. I loved them when I was younger and old habits die hard," I admit with a shrug.

"Tell me, then, what's it going to take to fully convert you to the good side? Even the World Series victory last year wasn't enough?" His diamond-studded ring glints in the light from the streetlamps along my block.

I flash back to that glorious game—and the night I started having dirty dreams about Chance. I was at the ballpark for the game, and I'd hugged him after the win. His divorce had just been finalized and he was fully single, so maybe that's why I started thinking about him in all new ways after one celebratory embrace.

"Fine," I say. "Winning it all last year did help a smidge."

We stop in front of my place. "Then, Sierra, I will just have to keep trying to convince you."

His eyes flicker with mischief.

Perhaps, dirty mischief?

Ohhh. I hope that's a yes. That my people-reading skills are on the ball right now.

Because even in the dark, I'm pretty sure I can read

heat in his eyes—speculation in the way they travel up and down my body. The man wants me to ask him up.

And holy hell.

I want to invite him in.

No more noodling over possibilities, no more wondering.

I like the way he looks at me—*a lot*. His hot gaze sends a zing down my body.

We're on the brink of something. A crossroads in our friendship where maybe we both want it to go to the next level.

Only, I want to be absolutely positive.

Don't want to make a mistake. To misread a man again.

I'm the opposite of impulsive. I plan my outfits down to my panties. I schedule my days and the drinks I'll make at night. And I definitely don't jump into bed with men.

Even though, I'm pretty sure I finally know where I want all this attraction with Chance to go. I can see the destination and I want to savor the journey. Each fun, flirty step to the bedroom for the very first time.

"Yes, you should keep trying," I say, officially flirting.

"Then I will," he says, giving it right back.

I wiggle my fingers in goodbye. "Good night, Chance. Good luck in the playoffs. Maybe I'll root for you."

He hums, tossing me a crooked grin. "Maybe I'll stop by The Spotted Zebra again."

"Ah, now you're being convincing."

"That's exactly what I want to be," he says.

And his arms are exactly what I want to feel around me.

So, I slide in for a quick hug, enjoying his warmth, the woodsy clean scent of him. I linger for a little longer and, oh yes, he does too.

When he ends the hug, he gestures to where my blonde hair curls over my shoulder. "By the way, nice pink streak. Glad you changed it from Dragons purple."

Reflexively, I lift a hand, smoothing the splash of color.

"But pink isn't the Cougars color," I point out.

"But it's not the Dragons color anymore either. So, I'll take it as a sign to keep up my *Be a Cougars Fan* campaign," he says with a grin.

"Keep campaigning, Chance."

"Count on it," he says, his voice a little husky.

"And thank you for walking me home. You're a good guy," I say as I push open the door to my building.

"And I'm a convincing one," he says.

And as of tonight, I think he could be a promising one.

It's a late September evening, and with the way his eyes sparkled in the night, I'm pretty sure I know who I want to be my first.

The man walking away from me.

2

CHANCE

A few weeks later

My favorite way to finish a game?

Record a save.

My least favorite?

Sitting on my ass and twiddling my thumbs because my team doesn't even need to call me to the bullpen to warm up.

I'm slumped over on the bench in the world's quietest dugout. It's October, the seventh inning of game six of the divisionals.

The Cougars don't need me to save the game since there's no win to save. We are down by a grotesque nine runs.

Yup. The Texas Scoundrels are clobbering us in our home park in front of forty thousand fans.

Unless fortune smiles on us in a big way, I won't be

going to the bullpen. I won't be doing anything but heading home far too early in the postseason.

Two innings later, the Scoundrels' closer shuts down the big bats in our lineup, the team advances in the playoffs and celebrates on our diamond.

I curse along with my teammates. Safe to say there are no happy campers among the Cougars tonight. We won the World Series last year, but the clock starts over every season. This time, we failed in our one and only goal—to be the last men standing.

I trudge to the locker room, shower, get dressed, then gather my shit. The season is officially over.

But one of my rules is: *don't be a sore loser.*

Stay strong.

I man up, clap my teammates on their backs, and tell them it was a good year. The guys and I exchange a bunch of halfhearted *see you next years,* and *have a good off-seasons,* and then I head to the door.

I make my way through the corridor of the ballpark then out into the San Francisco night, leaving the game behind.

Once I'm outside, I scan for a familiar face—one I see in the mirror every morning. Ah, there he is. My twin brother leans against a lamppost, AirPods in, singing under his breath.

TJ is the king of finding new, obscure bands nobody's heard of, so I don't bother asking what he's listening to—I won't have a fucking clue.

He takes his earbuds out and offers, with sympathy, "Want me to pretend I'm you so you don't have to hear every single person we're about to see tell you how bummed they are by the loss?"

I perk up. Now *that* is a save. "Yes. Fucking yes."

"Consider it done."

TJ calls a Lyft, and a few minutes later we slide into the Prius that arrives for us. In the backseat, we trade shirts, a necessity since TJ dresses better than I do. I'm the king of T-shirts and pullovers, but as a writer, my brother can pull off a cool hipster style. That's how I find myself wearing a short-sleeved beige shirt in a fabric patterned with cartoonish mushrooms—psychedelic ones, I'm sure—in shades of orange and brown and yellow.

"You do know I hate mushrooms," I point out.

"Good. Then the shirt is ironic too," he says, then gestures to my gray T-shirt. "And I hate boring clothes. So we're even."

"Fair enough." I take a quick glance at TJ in my clothes.

Almost there.

I tug my World Series ring off my finger and give it to him with a warning. "Be nice to my precious."

"Of course, Gollum." TJ slides the beauty on, the symbol of one of my greatest professional accomplishments. He waggles his hand, letting the diamonds and sapphires catch the streetlights as the car cruises to the Mission. "Thank you, little bro. And see you later. I have an auction to attend. Gonna see if I can find me a buyer for this bad boy."

I slam a hand on his shoulder. "And if you do that, I

won't hesitate to tell all your adoring fans that you don't actually believe in happily-ever-afters."

Growling, he narrows his dark eyes. "Blasphemy! You wouldn't dare."

"Just try me if you fence my ring."

A few minutes later, the Lyft arrives at The Lucky Spot in the Mission. "Thanks, man," I say to the driver, then we head into the bar. Normally, I'd go to The Spotted Zebra after games with my teammates. But if I do, I'll flirt with the bartender, and that's not cool to do when my big brother—by five minutes—is in town.

Once inside, I ask for a booth, and the host does a double take.

"Mr. Ashford?" he asks, his eyes flicking from TJ to me and back.

TJ and I point at each other.

We both laugh. Can't help it.

Our twin swap still cracks me up. It cracked us up when we were five years old and tricked our parents at dinner.

We fooled teachers at school too, when we were in the mood to be little jackasses.

Our tricks were harder to pull off as we grew older and developed different talents. Since I couldn't send him in to sub for me on the mound, and he couldn't lean on me to sign books for fans while chatting about their favorite kissing scene in his romantic tales, we don't have many chances to play the old switcheroo.

But this right here is the perfect moment.

"I'll show you to your booth. That was a tough loss," the host says to TJ as he guides us through the bar.

"Yeah, that was such a bummer. I cried in the dugout," TJ says as me, with such a beleaguered sigh, I kind of want to smack him.

"Dude, I cried too," the host says as we reach the booth.

My brother slides in. I sit across from him, glad to be out of the crossfire of random fan sympathy even as TJ hams it up with his reply: "Baseball is life. All I wanted was to bring life back into that game tonight."

"I'm telling you, if you'd have gotten in, Chance, we'd have locked that series up. Sent the Scoundrels packing back to Texas," the host says.

"You bet your San Francisco Cougars ninety-eight-mile-an-hour fastball ass my bro would have shut them down," I put in.

TJ strokes his bearded jaw. Damn good thing I grew out my beard in the postseason. TJ and I match completely. "I had my best pitch all lined up too," he says. "I was ready to throw fire from my hands like the Devil himself."

The host smiles sympathetically. "I wish you'd been able to break out your cutter, Chance," the guy says. "I still remember when you struck out that Miami Ace last year. Don't let this time get you down though. You are our World Series champions, and we will always love you."

TJ affects a choked-up sob, clasps his heart. "Means the world to me. Thanks, man."

The host turns my way, flashes a courteous grin. "You must be the romance writer."

"Roses are red, violets are blue, romance is awesome,

except when it's not," I quip, and holy fuck it's hard to come up with rhymes on the spot.

TJ lowers his head, laughing. "Please tell me that's not going in your next book."

I grin wider. "You know what I am going to put in my next book? A guy who has really big feet. He wears really big shoes. His name is going to be . . ."

"Longfellow?" the host asks, helpfully.

"Nope. Bigfoot," I say deadpan.

The guy laughs, then hands us the menus. "Let me know when you're ready, Mr. Ashford and Mr. Ashford," he says, then sets a sympathetic hand on TJ's shoulder. "Until next season."

The man smiles and walks away.

I stare at my brother with an arched brow. "Seriously? You cried in the dugout?"

"Just be glad that I waxed on and on about your sport instead of saying roses are red and violets are blue. Also, I am not putting Bigfoot in my book."

"But I bet your hero will have *big feet*," I say, sketching air quotes.

"All romance heroes have *big feet*. That's like saying he'll have carved abs and drink scotch."

"Wait. You mean he'll look just like me?" I ask, then yank up the mushroom shirt and flash my six-pack.

TJ rolls his eyes. "You're so modest, Chance. Don't let anyone ever tell you that you aren't a paragon of humility."

"I won't," I say.

TJ leans back in the booth, a slow and satisfied grin spreading on his face. "It worked."

"What worked?" I ask.

TJ points at me. "Me playing you. It got your mind off the game."

I smile. "It did. Thanks. Appreciate it." I sigh heavily. "I know I have no right to be upset, but damn, I wanted to advance."

"Course you did. You're a take-no-prisoners competitor. Losing sucks, no two ways about it. But at least there are burgers and beer."

"And that'll have to do," I say, then peruse the menu.

When the server swings by, we order, and once he leaves, TJ dives into music talk, telling me about a new band he's into called Secret Frog Lovers Mate in the Night.

"What is it about bands these days? Why can't they just have normal names?" I ask.

"There are no normal names anymore," he says.

I snap my fingers. "Normal Name. That would be a good name for a band."

TJ arches a brow. "You sure about that? Would you listen to a band called Normal Name?"

He has a point. "No, but only because, unlike you, I already listen to music artists people have heard of. Shawn Mendes. Justin Timberlake. Post Malone."

"Word of advice—either develop taste or turn to me for playlists to impress the ladies."

Another excellent point, but I won't concede. "Yeah, count on that never. Besides, I've had no lady to impress in ages."

He nods in understanding, then asks, "Anyway, what are your plans for the off-season?"

"I've got a couple events with sponsors in the next few weeks before I go to New York in November for a big shoot with a watchmaker. I'll be the new face of Victoire watches."

"Do you mean you'll be the *new wrist* of Victoire?"

"Pretty sure they want this face too," I say, gesturing to my cheek. "We're a package deal."

"Want me to fill in, since I'm the more handsome one? I could probably sell more watches than you."

"Speaking of modesty," I say, laughing. It's true—no one takes my mind off bad games like my brother.

The server stops by with our beers; we thank him, then we toast to French watchmakers and big feet.

"Anyway, the watch thing sounds like a sweet gig," TJ says after he sets down his beer. "Are you going right after the wedding?"

No clue what he's talking about. "What wedding?"

The golden flecks in TJ's brown eyes glimmer. "Blake's wedding," he says. "Cousin Blake. Mom's sister's son. Blake, the Hot Tub King."

Ohhhhhhhhh.

I groan, put the glass on the table, and slump down in the booth. "Yes, I know who Cousin Blake is, but seriously? He's getting married *next* month?"

"Yes. The save-the-date cards were sent out ages ago," TJ says.

"I know, I know. But I haven't received my invite yet, and my brain erased it." I drag a hand over my face. "In fact, it was preventing a horrible future memory. It's like the start of a reward. It's a pre-ward. My brain was giving me a pre-ward for forgetting it."

TJ holds up a wait-a-minute finger then grabs his phone, dictating into it. "Book note: character makes a joke about a pre-ward before he gets a sex *re*ward."

"Hey! I want royalties for that."

TJ winks. "Sure. You can have them when you give me ten percent of your bank for all the times I caught fastballs in the backyard growing up. Anyway, Blake's a good guy. He's fun. He's the life of the party, and he's using all that hot tub dough to host a sweet tropical destination wedding for him and Trish. Why don't you want to go?"

I stare at my brother. He can't be serious. "Gee, can you think of a single reason I don't want to go? Like, maybe . . . a bridesmaid?"

Realization dawns at the mention of my ex-wife's role in the wedding. "Shit, man. I genuinely did forget about that. Want me to pretend to be you?" he offers.

I press my hands together in prayer. "Please. Would you go as me?"

TJ stares at the ceiling, maybe considering it, then lets out a sad sigh. "I would. There's only one little problem. I already RSVP'd, so Blake and Trish know *I'll* be there," he says, tapping his chest. "If I go as you, I'm the asshole—me, as in TJ—who didn't show."

"Got it. Makes sense. But man, I do not want to see Natasha." There's no way around that. We're all interconnected—Blake, Natasha, and me. Trish, the bride, is my ex-wife's stepsister, and Natasha introduced her to Blake, my cousin, at one of my baseball games.

Natasha, who ran me through the wringer in our divorce.

Who did her best to paint me as the distant, absent, always-on-the-road spouse.

And since I didn't want to draw any more media attention to my imploding personal life and her very public *lament for the end of her marriage to All-Star Major Leaguer Chance Ashford,* all I could do was keep my head down and ride it out.

Even when, a week before the divorce was finalized, I learned she'd been cheating on me for the past three years.

The irony is enough to make anyone bitter. Natasha's a lifestyle coach and purveyor of platitudes under the brand *Notes to Self.*

Our split gave her endless inspiration. Nothing like seeing the private details of your disintegrating marriage on Instagram, captioned with banal affirmations over a picture of a breakfast smoothie. If I never again see a filtered photo of avocado toast—*It's not selfish to care for yourself*—it'll be too soon.

Note to me: relationships suck.

"Look," TJ says, "if you really want, I can say something came up. I'll tell them my book is overdue—which is true—and my publisher is breathing down my neck—also true—and I just can't go. Then I'll go as you." My brother scratches his jaw. "Honestly, it might be a little cathartic getting to zing your ex-wife in your place. I can even come up with a whole list of digs, so I'm prepared."

I smile, grateful for the offer. But that's too much to ask anyone, even my twin. "Appreciate it, but I can't have you do that. Also, you hate Natasha, so you'd snap and then the jig would be up. Mom would be furious at both of us, and Dad would try to make everyone happy."

I shudder at the thought of ticking off either of them—or anyone, really.

"Just like they did when they split." TJ stares thoughtfully out the window. "Okay, scratch that. We don't need to deal with that again." Then he jerks his gaze back to me as if an idea jolted him. "You could take a date."

How do dates even work anymore? "I haven't had a date in a year. Are you taking someone?"

TJ scoffs. "No way. There's no dude I want to be holed up with in Hawaii for a weekend. Romance and me broke up. I am single all the way. Like, in perpetuity."

"Perpetually single is the way to go," I say, offering a fist for bumping.

Our burgers arrive, and after a few delicious bites, I set down the food, a fantastic thought dipping into my brain. "Maybe my invitation was lost. Or maybe Blake isn't inviting me on account of Natasha being there. Maybe he's being pre-thoughtful? That's possible."

TJ smiles as he chews. "You've always been the big dreamer between the two of us."

I shrug, owning it. "I'm going to hold on tight to this dream. I am going to cup it in my hands and squeeze it until it comes true."

* * *

I dream that the invitation was lost in the mail. I wish that it were sent to Mars. I imagine an eagle swooped down and plucked it out of the mail carrier's bag like a fish from a river. But my dreams die a painful death when I open the mailbox a few days later after returning from a morning workout. Outside my home in Pacific Heights, my hands clasp a white envelope. With embossed writing, my name in silver taunts me.

Three days in Maui.

Three days seeing Natasha with the man she left me for. The man she cheated on me with.

Three days with family asking how I'm doing, if I'm sad, how I'm handling the end of my marriage, if I'm moving on.

The answer? I've moved on, closed up the heart, and taken myself out of the falling-in-love rotation.

But I'd rather not see their sympathetic faces. Hear the *good for yous*.

My chest tightens with knots, like how I feel when I face a terrifying batter. A leftie with tree trunks for arms.

But do I back away from vicious lefties who try to chew up closing pitchers like they're chicken bones?

Nope.

I stare down those fuckers and throw them the nastiest stuff.

I snap the invitation against my palm, TJ's advice ringing loud and clear in my ears.

Take a date.

It's not a bad idea.

After keeping on my game face while Natasha, her

adoring fans, and random strangers painted me as the bad guy, I'd like to let the world know I've moved on. I've finally climbed out of the "smile and wave as my marriage implodes on social media" phase of my life, and I don't want to go down that road again.

Showing up to support my cousin despite Natasha being in the wedding party will let the world know I'm a good sport.

Hell, I'm a goddamn good guy.

Just like I've always wanted to be.

All I need is a date for the wedding.

But asking the woman I have in mind will require some finesse and a little research.

Time to see what Google has to say on the subject.

3

SIERRA

Today calls for . . . fuchsia.

It's my sixth, twenty-ninth, or maybe one-hundredth day in a row running on coffee and determination, but I'm giving exhaustion the middle finger while blasting Ariana Grande as I get dressed for work.

You know what? This day doesn't just call for fuchsia.

It requires a fuchsia satin bra with a black bow between the breasts.

I grab that sexiest of sexy numbers from the padded hanger in my closet, snap it on, and consider my reflection.

"Sierra Blackwood, you get a thumbs-up for your devotion to satin," I tell myself as my playlist switches to Katy Perry.

Girl power.

It's what I need to conquer the night.

I tug on a black T-shirt that slopes off one shoulder and shows off the cherry tree ink on my arm—always a perfect conversation starter with patrons—pull on skinny jeans, then slide into a pair of black leather ankle boots and I'm ready to go.

In the living room, I grab a leather jacket and my purse. Tom dozes luxuriously on the purple couch—my big tuxedo rescue does *cat* incredibly well. Scratching his soft chin, I coo, "Don't look so happy. You'll make me jealous, love."

He stretches his neck, giving me even more room to stroke his chin. "Hedonist. That's what you are."

My main man purrs like an earthquake, then stretches his legs out in all directions. "I swear you're mocking me," I tell him.

Watch me . . . sleep. Watch me . . . rest. Watch me . . . do nothing.

I'd like to be reincarnated as my cat.

What? Where did *that* come from. He's a man of leisure. I'm a woman of work. What would I even do if I were brought back as the king of relaxation?

Nice thought though.

Definitely a nice thought.

"I'll miss you tonight." I kiss his furry black and white head, then grab my keys, stopping along the way to the door to sniff a vase of orange calla lilies. Mmm. These smell soft and clean, with hints of jasmine.

But there's no time to linger.

I grab a stick of cinnamon gum and pop it in my mouth as I leave my building and walk to work. The sharp, strong flavor is like a hit of adrenaline. A damn necessary one too.

When I reach The Spotted Zebra, I spit out the gum

in a trash can, unlock the door to my bar. Even though I'm running on fumes, I relish the quiet as I head behind the bar, set down my purse, and then seize the few minutes of solitude to whip up some cocktail chemistry.

Ever since that night he walked me home, I've had the idea to create a new drink – liquid courage, so to speak.

For me.

I haven't been able to stop thinking of Chance, and all the things I want to do with him. Over the past few weeks, I've been snagging time here and there to perfect a new drink.

Making it bolsters my confidence. I'm in my element crafting cocktails—playing with liquors and mixes, with measurements and proportions.

And hell, will I ever need an extra dose of confidence when I finally see him again.

When I ask him my question.

As I stir in the tequila, I'm pretty sure I've finally got the perfect mix.

I take a small sip.

Mmm. Yes.

This is the "please take my V-card" drink.

It's sweet and bold, everything I need to ask a question that has my nerves jumping like grasshoppers.

But a good drink should settle me.

Perhaps it's time to nudge this along.

I grab my phone and tap out a text. Nothing too bold. Just a simple note, serving the ball into his court.

Sierra: I'm still not sold on the benefits of being a Cougars fan.

Seconds after I hit send, three dots appear.

Chance: I'm working on a very convincing argument. I promise to stop by and wow you with it.

A burst of excitement flares inside me. Maybe he'll swing by tonight. If he does, I'll say damn the butterflies and serve him this drink. Then, I'll finally woman up and ask him to help me out of my lingerie sometime.

Sometime very soon.

* * *

A few hours later, the joint is jumping, just the way I like it. Alt-rock plays at the perfect volume to soundtrack a conversation, but not so loud as to require yelling. Patrons lounge on black-and-white striped couches and pink chaise lounges. A chalkboard menu lists my signature drinks, as well as my new creation, which I also posted on Instagram.

At the bar, I slide the concoction to Trish. I call it *Wild Chemistry*, and it's a little bit tequila, and a little bit tropical, and a lot sexy. As she reaches for the glass, she flicks her jet-black waves from her shoulder, parts her perfectly lip-glossed pink lips, then declares, "This is the best."

"You haven't even tried it yet," I say, giving a smile to

one of my most loyal patrons. A woman who put my bar on the map. I love her madly.

"Doesn't matter," Trish says with a breezy shrug, then shows the variation on a piña colada to our friend Clementine. "How much do you want to bet this will be the best cocktail ever?"

Clementine drums silver fingernails on the counter then dips her pretty voice to a stage whisper. "I won't bet against Sierra. Her drinks are the bestest of the best. Plus, I had a *Wild Chemistry* before you arrived, Trish, and they're divine."

"Shhh. Don't tell her all our secrets," I say to Clementine Rose, whose name is the perfect kind of perky for the elite pet trainer with a renowned client roster, and a year-long waiting list. The pixie cut and a whirling dervish of a personality complete the promise of her name.

"Clem, you started celebrating Thursday night without me." Trish pouts.

Clementine did indeed start early, and now she's returned to her signature drink, so she lifts a martini in a toast. "Yes, I did! Because Thursday is a fabulous night, and I always have great dreams on Thursday because tomorrow is Friday. Like, dreams where my star Chihuahua pupils perform pirouettes, or I ride a Pegasus across the sky."

And I think I just growled in jealousy. "Those are your dreams?"

She beams. "Yes, but sometimes I also have simpler dreams. Just your average fantasies. Like, say, there's a revival of *Chess* on Broadway starring Hugh Jackman and I have front-row seats."

I wish. "Oh, yeah, that."

Trish rolls her eyes. "Can I have your dream rather than the one I had last night where the seamstress tailored my wedding dress to . . . *vaginal length.*"

Clementine cringes. "That's terrible. But just think positive thoughts before bed, Trish, and you'll be fine."

I clear my throat. "I beg to differ. I think about sex before bed, and I still dream that I'm late for the first day of school, stumbling into English class with my teeth falling out and no underwear on, not knowing the lines to the sonnet I had to memorize. Or I show up at The Spotted Zebra well past happy hour and customers are lined up outside, tossing overripe bananas at the window."

Clementine blinks, her jaw falling open in horror. "Girl, that's not a dream. That's a nightmare."

"I know," I say, crinkling my nose.

Trish sets a gentle hand on mine. "But that's also a sign you're working too hard, Sierra."

I shrug, dismissing the notion. It's just a dream. And if dreams meant something, I'd be running from zombies all day long too.

"You're always here, though," Clementine adds, concern etched in her green irises. "It's like I tell the companions of the dogs I train—you have to rest, or you won't be a good dog person."

"And nothing is more important than being a good dog person," Trish says, reciting Clementine's business logo.

"Except hiring good talent who can help you be a rock star," Clementine says lifting her glass high in a rocker salute and somehow still managing not to spill a single drop. Then she sets down her martini and turns to the bride. "All right, Miss Miyoshi, but not for long," she says to Trish. "Let's catch up on all the plans. Do you have everything you need for the big day?"

"I think I do." Trish rattles off wedding plans as I scan the bar. Spotting a goateed patron in need of a refill, I head over and mix him another gin and tonic, making small talk. I'm proud of the establishment I've built in only three years. Proud, especially, that my Major League baseball brother loaned me the money to buy this bar and it's been successful enough to pay him back in less than three years.

This place is all mine now.

A lot of that has to do with Trish, a benefactor of sorts who became a friend.

About two and a half years ago, the tastemaker among tastemakers strolled in, ordered a *Long-Distance Lover*, then talked up The Spotted Zebra on her cocktail review show that has about a gazillion YouTube followers.

I am so stinking lucky she discovered my place and fell in love with it.

Lucky, too, since she and her friends are pretty cool, and now they're my peeps too.

I hand the gin and tonic to the goateed guy, then swivel around to restock some liquor. But as I grab another bottle of gin from the back room, an SUV of a yawn drives into my mouth and parks there.

That's embarrassing. I hope no one saw that.

My eyes flutter for a second. Red spikes of pain needle them, that tired sensation. Maybe it's that conversation about dreams that's dragging me down.

That has to be it. A glance at the clock tells me it's only nine, and normally I've got gallons and gallons of energy to make it through a night.

I leave the back room, return to the bar, and mix a drink for another customer, who wants to know the best fun things to do in the city. The answer is easy-peasy. "You've got to try neon bowling at Pin-Up Lanes in the Marina and karaoke in Japan Town," I say, then it happens again. Another Subaru-size yawn I have to stifle.

What is wrong with me?

Work is my life force.

This bar is my fuel.

But when I return to chat more with Trish and Clementine, I feel like I'm in the hot back seat of a car on a long road trip, fighting to stay awake.

This is not the Sierra in fuchsia who kicks ass and takes names. This is not a woman wearing a black satin bow between her tits.

This is a woman who's . . . absolutely fucking zonked.

I can't remember the last time I took a day off. I'm sure it was in the Joe era, so, more than a year ago. A wasted day, since my ex turned out to be the worst.

I pour myself an iced tea, guzzle it, and power through the rest of the night, saying goodbye to Trish and Clementine when they take off.

My eyes are glued to the entrance of the bar the rest of the time, hoping Chance will want to wow me tonight.

Every time the door opens, I steal a glance until I start to feel like a stalker in my own bar.

By the time eleven rolls around, my shoulders sag. Fine, he didn't promise he'd make an appearance, but I do wish he'd swung by. I'm not bold enough to seek him out to ask my question. I want to do it on my home turf, where I feel naturally gutsy.

For now, I shove the baseball star from my mind. Besides, if he had come by tonight, I might have yawned in his fabulous face as I served him the *Wild Chemistry* and asked him to cash in my V-card.

He's the ideal man for my project. A man I know and trust. A man who's a friend. A man I'm attracted to. A man who doesn't seem keen on anything serious.

I finish up work, closing The Spotted Zebra at one. After I say goodbye to the last employee to leave, I check the inventory, then head to the black-and-white couch by the window. Curling up there, I tally the night's receipts on my laptop, then review my expansion plans for the bar as I watch the last of San Francisco go to sleep.

Soon, the streets are quiet.

And it's so comfy on this couch.

So cozy and warm in here.

The tables on this spreadsheet are just a little fuzzy. Maybe they'd be a little less fuzzy if I shut my eyes.

* * *

A bell clangs.

Rings loud and painfully in my ears.

Another one joins in. Like angry church bells in a movie scene with a chorus of clocks ringing.

My eyes fly open.

I've got to get to The Spotted Zebra.

Can't miss opening the bar.

Customers might be lined up.

Happy hour is such a busy time, and I can't be late. Because of the bananas. The overripe bananas.

Except, why is it so bright at happy hour?

Peering out the window, I startle as big blue eyes stare back at me in a cherub-like face framed by blonde ringlets. A tiara is perched on the hair of . . . a three-year-old?

I blink.

A little girl wearing a pink tutu is pointing at me, laughing, then tugging her mom's hand.

Bleary-eyed, I offer a pathetic smile and wave at the mom and young child walking past The Spotted Zebra on a Friday morning at seven.

Great. Just great.

I fell asleep at work.

And I slept for five and a half hours.

It's the most solid block of sleep I've had in . . .

Actually, I can't remember the last time I got five and a half hours in a row. With a yawn, I drag myself through the bar, grab my purse from my office, and root around for a toothbrush. I head into the bathroom and brush my teeth.

Yanking my hair into a true messy bun—there's

nothing artful about this nest on my head—I return to the couch, grab my laptop, and finish the work I left undone last night.

Then, I grab my purse, and lock up at the ridiculous hour of eight fifteen when I should be home, snug under my purple duvet, fighting off dreams of losing my teeth.

I don't even like to go to Pilates at this time of day.

I like to *sleep*.

As I walk, I pop my earbuds in to listen to one of my favorite female comedians riffing about her great accomplishment in adulting recently—buying a towel.

I laugh, wishing I were worried about how to buy linen. Instead, I'm obsessed with expansion plans.

When I turn the corner, I blink as the picture of perkiness comes into view. Platinum-blonde Clementine, who's bright-eyed and bushy-tailed in her sapphire blue yoga pants and matching top, is walking with her speed-demon Papillon.

She flashes a huge grin as she calls out, "Woman!"

"Woman to you," I say, a little half-heartedly.

My friend stops in front of me, parks a hand on her hip, then sizes me up in a split second. "I know your dirty little secret," she says, wagging a perfectly manicured finger. There's a tiny painted Papillon on the silver nail.

My face flushes for a hot second at the mention of my crush on my brother's teammate. "I know you do. But why are you bringing it up now?"

Clem tilts her head in question, her brow knitting. "Because look at you. You're wearing the same clothes as last night. You slept at the bar last night. And you're in big trouble."

Oh. That secret.

Not the *I want Chance to take me* one. I groan. "I suck. I know. What is wrong with me?"

"Well, for starters, you're married to the bar," she says matter-of-factly. "You work yourself to the bone because you're so damn focused on the next thing and then the thing after that. You don't date even after Joe turned out to be such a gigantic asshat. And you're horny. That's all."

Yes. That's all. I'm just on a path to burnout and I'm barely twenty-five. "And you dream of unicorns. Fuck you."

She pouts.

"C'mon. You know that was an affectionate fuck you," I say with as much of a smile as I can muster.

"Obviously. But I'm worried about you, Sierra," she says, then bends to pick up her brown and white pooch, who's waggling his paw at me. "And so is Magnus. We are very concerned."

I am too. Trouble is, I don't know how to combat exhaustion. I never learned that skill in my *do everything well for yourself since your parents sucked* crash course I've been taking for years.

I heave a sigh and shrug helplessly as I stroke Magnus's soft head. "Me too. But I don't know what to do," I say, since go-go-go is my speed.

"You need a vacation, Sierra," Clementine says. "No ifs, ands, or buts."

She's not wrong. But I can't afford to get away for

more than a night. I already moved heaven and earth to snag one night off for Trish's wedding in Hawaii.

I kind of can't wait for those twenty-four hours away from work.

Twenty-four hours in paradise.

"Maybe, but I don't know how to pull it off."

She taps her temple. "Leave it to your friend Clem. A plan is coming together. But now, I've got to work on Magnus's pole-weaving skills. Bye for now. More later."

With a wave, she heads toward her home, and I make my way to mine. As I go, my mind drifts to flowers and gardens and tropical scents. When I turn on my block, my brother's standing outside my building, decked out in running gear, stretching his quads, his T-shirt a little sweaty.

That's odd. Not the sight of Grant in motion, since that pretty much describes him, but his presence at my door.

"Are you stalking me?" I call out.

"Yes. It's my new hobby in the off-season."

"Cool. Mine is . . . talking to my cat and dreaming of Hawaii," I say drily.

"You and me both. Well, for the last one. Deck and I are going there in a few weeks." He's not going to attend Trish's wedding. He and his boyfriend are headed to Kauai for a well-deserved vacation several days before I take off for Maui.

"You've only told me twenty times," I say, then stop, quirking my head as I study my brother, trying to figure out why he's here. "What are you up to?"

"I just went for a run, and I'm going to meet Chance and some of the guys at the gym in about an hour."

But that doesn't answer the question. "So . . . were you just waiting for me to come home?"

Grant stares at me like I've lost my marbles. "Um, way to make your brother feel welcome. Hello? We had a breakfast date at eight-thirty. In between my run and the gym. You said to meet you outside your place."

I groan, drop my head in my palm. "I forgot. Also, I fell asleep at work. I suck."

He wraps an arm around me, gives me a gentle hug, but laughs too. "Girl, what am I going to do with you?"

It's a valid question.

One that's starting to weigh on me.

On the one hand, I've succeeded at not becoming my parents—I'm twenty-five, a business owner, a college graduate, and a virgin. My parents didn't go to college. They got pregnant in high school. They flitted from job to job. They avoided all responsibility. They left Grant and me with my mom's parents. Best decision they ever made, since my grandparents rock. But I don't want to risk a chance of being like my irresponsible folks.

So, I bust my ass every damn day.

Then at night, I fashion expansion plans.

Just in case it all goes belly up.

Yay me.

I'm also running on fumes.

Something's gotta give.

As Grant and I settle into a booth at the café around the corner and I peruse the offerings, I wish the answer were on the menu.

4

CHANCE

Google and I need to stop meeting like this.

The search engine knows far too much about me.

Like: *Is Tinder a good idea?*

Worst things that happened on Tinder.

How to cancel my Tinder account before I use it.

Like right fucking now because that shit is scary. Scarier than spiders.

Spiders that live in bathrooms.

Spiders that can kill you.

Are all spiders deadly?

Something to take my mind off spiders…Like, is dating even called dating anymore? Is it grabbing a coffee? Or is it…chilling? Hanging?

How to ask a woman to hang out with you.

Is there anything that sounds douchier than asking a woman to hang out with you?

Ohhhhh. Asking her to have low-key coffee.

Got it.

Thanks, Google.

But wait. There's one more thing to ask the engine of the Web.

How to ask a woman to be your wedding date when you haven't been on a date in ten years.

What the hell do I say to Sierra? I contemplated stopping by last night when she texted, but I need to get my talking points in order first. Wait. Is that what they're even called? Fuck, it's hard navigating dating terrain after a decade-long marriage.

I met my ex-wife at our freshmen orientation in college and we were together for more than ten years. I've never been on Tinder. I've never met a woman at a bar. I've never picked up a gal at the gym.

Hell, I've never banged a fan, since I've been steadfastly single for the last year, and monking it up.

And my brother was right. I need a date to the wedding. I try again with Google. And I get a lot more specific.

How to ask a woman to be your fake date at a wedding.

After all, I can't ask her for a real date. Team Bro Code Rules and all.

As I whip up protein pancakes for breakfast, Google serves up the simplest of solutions to my dating query —find an interesting conversation starter, be friendly, and most of all, be direct about the need for the fake date.

Piece of cake. I can do that no problem. I ponder great conversation starters as I eat.

Cocktails? No.

Baseball? She's probably had enough baseball talk to last a lifetime.

I glance around my place. Plants? Doubtful she wants to shoot the breeze about my green thumb.

I finish my breakfast and clean up, then water my succulents. "What would you do, Mariano?" But I answer my question quickly. "Of course that's what you'd do. You'd find a killer opening line."

Next, I feed the panda plant on the windowsill, then give some H2O to the aloe plant, Trevor Hoffman, then, the jade, Dennis Eckersley.

Three of the greatest closers of all time. I owe them all a huge debt, and I've got to represent the position. A closer can motherfucking close.

* * *

At the gym an hour later, with opening lines on my mind, I join today's workout crew. Grant's here, along with Shane Walker, a pitcher for the New York Comets, and Harlan Taylor, a wide receiver on the Renegades.

I move behind Grant on the bench press, spotting him as Harlan does squats.

"Question of the workout: What's the most embarrassing place you ever fell asleep?" Grant tosses out as he pushes up the weight bar.

I answer as I spot my catcher while he lifts. "I fell asleep at the barbershop the other week, getting a shave and a haircut. My guy is such a pro, though, he didn't even nick my chin while I did the head slump."

Shane chuckles as he lifts free weights in front of the mirror. "Thought for sure you were going to say while shagging," says the Brit.

"Spoken from experience?" I fire back. Shane—also a closing pitcher—has been in town visiting family, so we've adopted him as our workout buddy for the week.

"Bet that happens to you a lot, Shakespeare," Harlan quips as he switches to lunges. "Maybe try being better in bed."

Shane scoffs. "Please. If I were better, I'd attain god-like status in the sheets. As it is, women say sex with me is rather transcendent."

Grant sets down the bar, sits up, rubs his hands along his shorts. "Transcendent as in they have to escape to another plane of reality to make it through even your two pumps?"

The Brit laughs it off. "Even if I were a two-pumper, those two pumps would be enough to give her multiples from another world."

I shake my head. "You are too cocky even for a pro athlete, Shakespeare."

"And that level is pretty much maximum-ego already," Harlan says. "To answer your question—I fell asleep on Abby's giant teddy bear the other night."

I laugh at the mention of his young daughter. "That doesn't sound so odd. Cute, but not odd."

Harlan looks up, pauses his lunges, his brown eyes twinkling. "Oh, did I mention the teddy bear was in the living room and Abby had three kindergartners over, and they decided to paint Daddy's toenails while he was asleep."

We all crack up. When Harlan unties his sneaker and wiggles his rainbow-colored toes, we laugh harder.

"You've got a budding pedicurist on your hands," Grant says.

Harlan pats his light brown locks. "I'm just glad she's not a budding hairdresser."

The football player puts his sneaker back on as Shane scratches his chin then gestures to Grant. "And what's the most embarrassing place you've had a lie-in, Grant?"

"Dugout. In between innings last year. I was zonked from our travel schedule, so I caught a few winks while the end of the lineup was at the plate. Anyway, I guess it runs in the family. Sierra told me she crashed at work last night. Fell asleep on the couch at her bar."

Yes!

That's the perfect conversation starter to pop the *will you pretend to be mine at the wedding* question.

It's personal, it's fun, it says I know her.

I send her a text that I hope is flirty, and I don't even have to google how to flirt.

This'll be as easy as throwing a fastball for a strike.

5

SIERRA

On the way to work, I pop into my favorite florist, grab a bouquet of dahlias, and thank Frankie.

"You're the best with blooms," I tell the woman who owns the shop by my home.

"And you are aces with compliments," she replies.

I head to the bar, and when I set the pink dahlias on the counter, already the place feels even more like my home.

I smell the blooms and have just begun my prep for the evening when my phone pings with a text. It's in the Clementine and Trish chat.

Trish: I heard. I hereby officially am ordering you to spend two nights at my wedding instead of one. Who spends one night in Hawaii???? Only workaholic robots like YOU. Turns out our room block has an extra room, so I'm using it as a gift-y for you! You can't say no!

Clementine: I HAD A DREAM YOU SAID YES, SO I'M MAKING IT COME TRUE WITH MY MILES! MILES! I'M GIVING YOU MILES!

But I have so much to do to prep for my expansion. After Trish's wedding, I have an overnight trip to Vegas to check out a potential new hire. Plus, I already booked my ticket to Maui for her nuptials and made my plans. I fly in the night before, and I'll join the gals in the afternoon for hair and nail prep, then attend the ceremony and reception. I'll catch a red-eye home that night, sleep on the plane, and be back in San Francisco well in advance of happy hour.

I planned it to the minute.

I'm about to reply with a *thanks but I can't accept this* when my phone pings with another text.

Chance: Save the best seat at the bar for me tonight—I'll be stopping by later. Let the great Cougars convincing begin. P.S. Are you still going to Trish and Blake's wedding?

I am, I am, I am!

Because I have no game, I write back stat.

Sierra: I've got Maui on my mind. And you know I always save the best seat for you. Let's see if you can convince me.

Chance: Just as a tease—the Cougars have awesome

hats. And on that note, I'll count down the hours till this evening. Look for me around eight-thirty.

My stomach flips. *A time*. He gave a time. Who gives a time unless he's flirting?

Who says he's *counting down the hours* unless he feels a spark too?

I don't believe in signs, except maybe *this* one.

Maybe I should say yes to Trish and Clem. What if I *can* swing one more night in Hawaii? One more night where this man will be.

Could that night be my opportunity with Chance?

I turn around and hunt for my manager, Zoey. She's at the chalkboard, writing the names of the drink specials, her red hair piled high in an artful bun. "Zoey, what are the chances you could fill in for me—"

"Yes."

"But you don't even know when—"

"Yes. It's a blanket yes."

She lowers her arm. With chalk in hand, she sets her palm on my shoulder. "Sierra, you need a break. Whenever you need me to fill in, the answer is yes."

So, it's that obvious.

Huh.

Maybe this trip is everything I need to recharge.

And to finally have sex.

A twofer?

"Thank you," I say, then give her the date.

"Consider it done."

The stars are aligning, and all I have to do is take a

big breath and lay my panties on the line with the man I want.

I write back to Trish and Clem and tell them I'll take them up on their fabulous offer.

* * *

At 8:28, the door swings open.

Chance strides in, taking up all the space in my mind.

Dark, wavy brown hair. A bearded jaw that I bet would feel fantastic rubbing against my face, and elsewhere. And that smile. Confident, and a little dirty.

My skin flashes hot.

Should I ask him my big question tonight or at the wedding? If I ask him in Hawaii, we both might be feeling the Maui magic as the ocean waves gently loll against the shore. The soft night breeze will kick up the scent of tropical flowers and the sea as we grab champagne and toast to the happy couple. Then I can ask the man if he'd please deflower me.

I've known he's the one I wanted since the night he walked me home.

I don't want to have a one-night stand with a stranger. I want the first man I sleep with to be a guy I like. But he should also be a guy who won't expect anything more.

I'm married to work. I have nothing more to give.

Chance is the same with his job. That makes him perfect for my *I'm ready* plans.

Just the thought of what he might do to me in bed

sends a hot shiver through me, reminding me what I'm wearing.

Black lace.

If he only knew what I wanted him to do to my lingerie.

As he heads to the bar, he flashes me a smile that's both sexy and sweet. He holds a pink cap in his hand, and I'm pretty sure that's for me.

Screw waiting. I'm going to ask the man tonight.

6

CHANCE

I shower that evening. I want to look my best when I make my be-my-date-with-a-twist request, so I tug on a gray Henley, since that's what the guys in TJ's books usually wear.

The one universal theme in the books—well, besides love conquers all and everyone likes big cocks—seems to be that dudes look best in Henleys, so I am decked out in my finest.

I leave my place with enough time to make a pitstop at the Cougars team store. I don't need Google to tell me to show up with a gift. That's just common sense. I grab something that makes me think of Sierra, catch a Lyft to Hayes Valley, then get out at The Spotted Zebra.

I'm a man on a mission.

But as I push open the door, I'm greeted by an upbeat love song and…the quickening of my pulse. Sure, it's been a long ass time since I've been on the market. But I've got this, so I talk back to doubt.

Dude, you threw the final pitch in the World Series a year ago. That can't be tougher than asking a woman to be your wedding date.

Gift in hand, I make my way to the bar, catching Sierra's gaze as I go. Her brown eyes laser in on me, flickering with mischief. Like something is on her mind too.

She gestures to the stool in front of her. "The best seat in the house."

"It definitely is," I say as I grab the stool, flash her a grin, and set down the gift. A pink Cougars cap with the big cat logo in sparkles.

"A Cougars hat. And it is *fine*."

"It matches your streak, and the sparkles are badass like you."

She dons the hat and models it like a pro. "Don't you just know the way to my heart—calling me a badass."

I pump a virtual fist. Yes, I can do this. "What can I say? I call 'em, like I see 'em, and I'm pretty sure you're a badass babe."

"Oh, stop, stop. I won't switch allegiance so easily."

I lean closer, lower my voice. "Have I mentioned we have the best closing pitcher in all of baseball? A team needs a man who can seal the deal."

And I'm gonna be that guy tonight too.

Her breath catches. "So does a woman."

Oh yes. I like that response a lot. "So, I've convinced you to root for the Cougars?"

She leans in close too, her voice feathery. "You're getting there."

"Excellent. And I hope I'm not breaking the rules by

showing up without my teammates," I say, my tone making it clear that I'm enjoying their absence.

The fiery blonde behind the bar arches a brow, slaps a napkin in front of me, then says, "Depends on whether you like breaking rules, Chance Ashford."

"Maybe I like bending them too," I say.

"Do you now?" Sierra parks her palms on the bar, a move that has the fortunate effect of pushing up her tits. Mmm. Tits. The ultimate distraction, but hey, so's a runner on second base.

I maintain my flirting focus. "But breaking them can be fun too," I add.

"Then, you can be a rule bender or breaker at The Spotted Zebra anytime. Now, what can I get for you? Lager? Gin and tonic? The Best Mojito in the City?"

She just rattled off my last three drink orders. That has to be a good sign she'll say yes to my request. "Someone remembers what I order."

Her lips curve into a grin. "Well, I *am* a bartender. There's also my new drink to consider. *Wild Chemistry*," she says, sounding even flirtier when she names that cocktail.

"What would you recommend?"

"Whatever you like."

Your company in Hawaii for a couple days. That's what I'd like.

But I've got to ease into my unconventional request, and a drink would smooth the way. Drumming my fingers on the bar, I flash back to TJ's last book. What did the hero drink? Ah, yes. He asked for scotch, naturally. As a hero does—Scotch, Henleys, and big cocks.

"Scotch please," I say, then add smoothly, "Macallan."

Her grin widens. She leans even closer, so damn close I catch a faint whiff of her body lotion or shampoo —blackberry. "Has someone been reading *Come Again*?"

Busted. And I like it.

"C'mon. Easton Ford can't be the only man who asks for a Macallan," I say, naming the hero from that book.

She smiles, sets a hand on my arm. "I'm just giving you a hard time."

I'd like to give her a hard time.

Except...This is a fake date request. You don't hookup with a teammate's sister. A teammate's sister is the kind of woman you take home to meet your mom. Time to settle the fuck down.

"Hard times are good," I say, and that feels like just the right amount of flirt for our…situation.

"One Macallan coming right up," she says, then pours a couple fingers worth.

A quick scan of the bar tells me it's now or never. The place isn't too crowded yet. She has other servers handling other patrons.

When she sets the glass in front of me, I whip out my conversation starter. "So, Sierra, word on the street says napping is your favorite hobby," I say playfully.

She tilts her head, puzzled, then awareness flickers in her eyes. "Oh my God, did my brother tell you what happened?"

I shoot her a grin. "Grant did indeed. He just can't keep secrets."

"I can't believe he told you that. But I also can't believe I fell asleep here. It was so embarrassing." She points to the couch by the window. "I woke up at seven with a little girl and her mom pointing at me like I was an animal at the zoo."

"I'm a big believer in naps. Relaxation is a very good thing."

"It wasn't a nap, Chance. It was a full-on Rip Van Winkle session," she says, then she takes a beat, flicks some blonde strands off her shoulder, and seems to shift gears. Her voice even goes a little smoky. "And, for the record, I'd much prefer to have been sleeping soundly on satin sheets wearing a lace teddy."

Hello! Did she just say what I think she said? "A lace teddy?" I ask, a little gravelly. Or maybe a lot gravelly.

"Or a nightie," she says, with a coquettish shrug.

My throat is the Sahara right now. Lifting my glass, I knock back some of the liquor. Setting the glass down, I clear my throat. "So I have a proposition for you. About the wedding."

Her soft-brown eyes flicker with excitement. "Oh good, because I have one for you. Also about the wedding."

I gesture to the floor so she knows it's hers. "Ladies first, after all."

She straightens her shoulders, then removes her hat, setting it behind the bar. Taking a glance around the room, she seems to assess the situation, then swings her gaze back to me. She parts her lips, like she's about to say something, but seems to reconsider it. "Actually, you go first."

That seems fair enough. A gentleman should ask, especially since she seems nervous. Squaring my shoulders, I dive into the deep end. "So, Trish and Blake's wedding. How would you feel about going as my date?"

A smile lights up her face as she says, "I would feel great." She nibbles on the corner of her lips, and I take that as a sign to serve up the rest of the details.

"But like a pretend date. No pressure or anything like that," I finish, wishing Google had better instructions for this request, but I'm winging it, and hoping for the best.

She's quiet for several long seconds. "Ah, we'd fake date."

"It's sort of an ex emergency," I explain. "I thought since I'm going and you're going, maybe we could go together. Natasha is one of the bridesmaids, and I would love to be with . . . a friendly face. The divorce was pretty brutal online—at least, the way she painted it on her feed. Everyone's going to ask me a ton of questions, and if I'm with you, they won't."

Doesn't hurt that Sierra is gorgeous, successful, and also fun as hell, but I'm not sure if I should say that yet. Google didn't shed any light on the nuances of pretend romance.

"Ohhhhh. You need a fake date," Sierra says.

"We can pretend to be together for the night. Maybe take a few pics. You'd help my social cred, which took a beating in the last year."

"Through no fault of your own," she says, crossing her arms, a tough girl vibe radiating off her.

That's just . . . hot.

"Thank you for saying that."

"Well, I don't like that she tried to portray you as a

callous ex-husband," Sierra says, and I bet she's wearing black leather boots to match her fiery attitude. A quick peek behind the bar confirms my suspicions, and damn, she looks good. "When we all know what really happened."

I tap my nose. "Bingo. That was *not* fun, smiling and waving like nothing bothered me."

But that was what my agent told me to do. *Best not to engage with Natasha. Keep your chin up and stay out of it,* Haven said.

I listened. I didn't engage.

Online, I kept my focus on baseball, volunteer work, my sponsors, and my friendships. And it worked. Staying out of the mess online helped me keep my sponsorships.

Sierra hisses, narrowing her eyes. "I wanted to punch every stupid Instagram post of hers, especially that one where she slapped up a shot of herself without makeup. *This is what starting over looks like. Being brave. Showing the world who you are.*" She gags dramatically.

I laugh, a little bitterly. "I distinctly recall Crosby telling me we were going to post a pic that day of the baseball game we played with kids for charity."

"Smart counter-strategy." She takes a deep breath. "So, the wedding is kind of the same."

"In a way, yes. Since I can't ask you out for real since you're Grant's sister," I add.

One pretty brow arches. "That's the issue? My brother?"

Well, the *other* issue is I have zero interest in relationships. Only good times. But I'd be a dick if I asked her to bang, especially since I need her help. "Bro code rules. Gotta follow them," I say.

"And the rules say you can't ask me out for real, but you can for pretend?"

"Bro code is a strange beast. It operates by its own rules. We could also just go as friends since we *are* friends."

She shoots me a look of fierce determination. "Damn straight we are. And so, as your friend, I say, fuck your ex-wife. You've got yourself a wedding date." She extends her hand.

"Great," I say, grinning wildly as we shake.

She lets go of my hand. "But the Blackwood code says I'm going to tell my brother we're pretend dates. Otherwise, he might hear, and then you'd have the *bro code* to answer to."

It comes out a little saucy, like maybe she's mocking the dude rules.

Honestly, the guy guidelines may deserve mocking, but without them, I'm pretty sure the Cougars would fall to pieces. After all, Grant is the guy I'm closest to on the team. He's the one who catches every single pitch I throw.

"Fair enough," I say. "No one wants *that*."

So, why do I feel unsettled? Maybe because she had something to ask me. I return to that. "By the way, what was your proposition?"

She takes a beat like she's trying to remember. "What do you know? I was going to ask the same thing. If you wanted to go as friends. Just friends. Nothing more. So, this whole pretend date works out perfectly."

And we're officially on the same page. Except it doesn't entirely feel that way and I'm not sure why.

I pick up my glass, drain it, and set it down.

"Want another?"

Scanning the board, I consider the options. Should I try the new drink she mentioned? "How's the *Wild Chemistry*?"

"Try it and find out," she says.

"I'll take a *Wild Chemistry*."

She spins around and whips up a cocktail, then sets it in front of me. I lift it and take a drink. "Mmm. It's a little tropical, and the tequila is just right. And is it crazy to say it tastes a bit sexy?"

Her lips twitch with the hint of a smile, then the smile disappears. "Not crazy at all."

"Is there a story behind the drink?"

She shakes her head. "Sometimes a drink is just a drink."

Sierra turns and heads the other way to help other customers, and soon I leave. I'm feeling both excited for our fake date, but also a little frustrated that it's not real.

Imagine that.

7

SIERRA

You don't always get what you want.

And you damn well don't cry about it.

"Do you, Tom?" I ask the next morning as I join my cat on his lounging couch.

Technically, it's *my* couch. But we both know the truth. His hair tells the story of ownership of this piece of furniture. Tom flops to his back, allowing for more belly rubs. I happily bestow them.

"See? You didn't caterwaul when I gave you organic chicken instead of the wild turkey that I know you prefer. But the organic chicken is better for your kitty belly," I say.

My man purrs louder, letting me know he understands how the world works. You get what you get, and you don't hiss about it.

"So I'm *not* upset that Chance didn't offer to toss me over his shoulder, carry me up here two steps at a time, kick the door down, then yank off all my clothes and bang me over the kitchen table," I tell the cat. "Are you?"

A louder purr is my answer.

Sure, I had other plans for him. But I said yes to Chance's fake date request because I know his pain.

Been there, done that.

Chance and I are kindred spirits in that department. We haven't talked about our pasts in detail, but I saw how Natasha spun self-care gold out of her divorce. More like a self-care empire of absolute bullshit.

I'm convinced there's a special kind of relationship torture waiting for people who cheat and lie. Like, maybe they can never have orgasms again.

Or maybe they're doomed to only kiss people who have wilted-lettuce breath. I certainly hope that's Natasha's fate.

And I hope my ex-boyfriend is racking up more than his fair share of limp lettuce lip-locks and blue-balled nights. If there's romantic justice in the universe, Joe's jeans will be too tight in the crotch for all eternity. Come to think of it, I'd like to wish an uncomfortable thong on Natasha for all her days.

If the tables were turned, and I needed a hot-as-sin, charming, wildly successful man by my side at an event, I wouldn't hesitate to ask Chance Ashford. And I'd march right into the thick of the party and show that hottie off like the arm candy, eye candy, and brain candy that he is.

That's what I'll do in Maui on our fake date, since cheating exes are the worst. My last serious boyfriend seemed as sweet as a cinnamon roll. Fitting that Joe was a baker, that supposedly adorable sweetheart of a man.

Turned out, the baker bamboozled the bartender.

I met Joe three years ago when we were both twenty-two, both virgins. We had a fantastic first date, strolling along the Marina, savoring the bay. We enjoyed several more fabulous dates with the swooniest goodnight kisses ever.

I wanted a little more. He said he wanted to wait until marriage. That was how he was raised, and it mattered to him.

Not my preference, but I'd waited twenty-two years at that point. I could wait longer.

Besides, I loved the guy. Loved his attention, the snickerdoodles he baked just for me, and his foot rubs.

Plus, our *almost-sex* life was mostly good enough.

Sometimes good enough.

Fine, some nights I was crawling up the walls. I desperately wanted to have sex. Would it be as hot, sexy, and naughty as I fantasized?

I was ready to find out finally. I'd held onto my V-card till my twenties because I'd made a promise to myself when I was in high school to live differently from my parents.

No sex in high school.

No sex in college.

And, evidently, no sex with Joe.

Then I discovered that after two years of *everything but* with him, he was giving *everything* to someone else.

Guess that was what mattered to him after all.

I kicked him out, cried ten rivers with Tom and my friends, then wiped my tears and buried my emotions in work, work, and more work.

Now, a year later, I'm well over Joe.

But I've also learned my lessons.

I have zero interest in dating. I don't want to get hurt. Don't want to get burned. And don't want to be made to feel a fool.

I am very interested in sex, though.

I'd like to feel pleasure. And I'm quite sure that knee-weakening, toe-curling, pull-my-hair, slap-my-ass-please sex would be the perfect cure to my burnout.

Yep. I've read books. I've watched dirty videos. I'm not afraid to explore my fantasies online, to check out all sort of adult content to learn what I like. I'm a subscriber to Joy Delivered's monthly O-box of battery-operated friends. This woman knows her mind and her body very much.

And I want that all with Chance Ashford.

But I also know this—I won't let an injustice take place on my watch.

So, fuck "Notes to Self" Natasha.

Fuck Cinnamon Roll Joe.

Even if Chance doesn't want a hot night with me because of a code, I'll gladly be his fake wedding date.

As I pet my cat, I send Grant a quick text.

Sierra: You know that wedding I'm going to in a couple weeks? Chance will be there as well, and I'm going as his date. But don't go all chest-thumping big brother on me. Don't spout the rules about dating a teammate's sister. His awful ex will be there, so we're only going to pretend to be dating so he can avoid the fire of dating questions.

Grant: I can't believe you think I'm a chest thumper.

Sierra: I can't believe you think you're anything but.

Grant: Look, I think it's cool that you're going to be by his side. And I don't have an issue with the whole teammate's sister thing. Just don't want to see you get your heart broken. Not by anyone. It's my job as your big brother to look out for you.

I laugh, rolling my eyes. He's such a big brother.

Sierra: You don't have a thing to worry about. My heart is not in the equation.

Because I won't let it be.

* * *

The next day, I power-walk with Clementine, though our pace is closer to a jog thanks to Magnus. He won a national dog agility competition last year that went viral and became known as Flying Magnus, the country's fastest little dog—busting records as he weaved through poles, raced through tunnels, and climbed up and down seesaws.

As we attempt to keep pace with Super Dog, I give my friend the download on the wedding date with Chance.

When we hit the corner of California, Clementine tugs gently on the leash, and Magnus sits instantly, waiting to cross till he gets a command. "You're going to pretend date the guy you've been lusting after? Just want to make sure I'm getting all the cray-cray details just right."

Is it crazy, though? Seems more like I'm being helpful. "Yes, but it's only for one event, and it's for solidarity."

With a laugh, she says *go* to the pooch, and we cross the street at a fast clip. "That is so sweet of you to provide a solidarity fake date to the guy you want to bang."

"That's what fake dates are. Expressions of solidarity and friendship. No one should face the inquisition of the ex alone."

"Ah, it's a great gesture of good will too?"

"I suppose it is."

"And will you dance with him?"

That's a good question. But it's a wedding. Hard to imagine we won't. "Probably."

Clementine bumps me with her hip. "Oh, baby. You'll get to feel that big, baseball body up against you. *Yum.*"

I roll my eyes. "Are you trying to tempt me?"

"I highly doubt I need to tempt you. I think you're already tempted, Sierra. Just imagine dancing with that hunk of a man when he's wearing a suit. Wait. Will he wear a suit to a Hawaii wedding? Oh, will he have a Hawaiian shirt on and linen pants? Who cares! Either will be smoking."

I try to picture what Chance might be decked out in,

and honestly, anything would look good on that man. "Exactly. He can wear whatever he wants."

"Athletes just look hot in *anything*."

"Does someone have a thing for athletes?"

Clementine bats her lashes, waves a demure hand. "You know there's a certain someone in my past. But it doesn't matter. I'm off the market, and we're talking about *you, you, you*," she says. "So you'll probably dance with Last Chance Train." That's the nickname sports talk hosts gave Chance years ago. Opponents like to say the last chance train is pulling out of the station when he takes the mound, since he's so hard to eke a hit off. "You'll shimmy with the hottie. Put a hand on one of those sexy biceps. He'll wrap his arm around you. Maybe you'll plant a kiss on his cheek."

She's painting an awfully alluring portrait of the wedding. One I doubt will bear any semblance to reality. I narrow my eyes at her. "Are you trying to drive me crazy?"

"Is it driving you crazy? I bet that's how you're going to feel at the wedding. Because that does sound kind of hot and bothery," she says as we march along Jackson Street.

I huff. "You're not helpful."

"I know. But, confession time—I'm more excited for your fake date with that hottie pants than I am for Trish's real wedding. And I'm ten thousand times excited for her. But don't you dare tell her I'm ten thousand and one times excited for you." Clementine wags a finger at me.

I mime zipping my lips. "I won't. And I'm glad you're

looking forward to my fake date, but I assure you there won't be a real one since he's Mr. Rules, and apparently his main rule is you don't date a teammate's sister." I heave a sigh, then raise a finger. "Wait. Idea. I'm going to temporarily emancipate myself from Grant."

My friend's green eyes sparkle with excitement. "Yes, girl, yes. I fully support you. This brotherly emancipation will be good for your lady parts. But you're still going to stay an extra night in Hawaii, right? You need it even for a hot fake date."

"You and Trish made a convincing argument. And really, I can't rush out at midnight. So yes, I will."

We reach the curb and stand stock still as Magnus sits like a proper dog. "You can laze around in a hammock. Watch a sunset. Take a dip in the pool."

That does sound appealing. "I'm glad you bullied me into the extra night. I'm looking forward to it."

Maybe not as much as I'd enjoy the room if it were the site of my fucking-for-the-first-time fantasies. But I'm pretty sure I'll enjoy being Chance's fake date too.

When we finish our almost-jog, I give Magnus a kiss on the head, then tell Clementine I'll see her soon.

She blows a kiss, then tells the dog to wave.

He lifts a tiny paw.

"Gah. Who needs a man when you have a perfect dog?" I call out.

She spins around, then spins back right in the middle of the crosswalk as a gray-haired lady passes her. "One more thing. Maybe consider telling Chance you want to bang him on his balcony."

My friend. Is she for real? As the lady snaps her gaze

back to Clementine, I try to rein in a laugh. "Could you be any louder?"

She cups a hand around her mouth. "Yes, I can!"

I stare at her, shaking my head, shrugging *sorry* at the woman who has probably suffered whiplash. "And no, I won't say that to him. Rules and all."

She shrugs airily. "Bet he'd do it. Bet he'd bend that one."

Bet I'd like to know.

8
CHANCE

A few weeks later

I might not be an expert on fake dates, but I'm familiar with a few key guidelines since I do read my brother's books from cover to cover. In *Mister Benefits,* when the hero needed a fake fiancée to pull off a business deal, he enlisted his female best friend. As part of the ruse, he booked a table at the best restaurant in the city for one of their dinners.

So, when Sierra tells me over text that her friends are using their miles to change her flight, I tell her I have more miles than anyone, and it would be my honor to upgrade her ticket.

Sierra: You don't have to do that.

Chance: I want to. And no fake date of mine is going to sit in coach when I'm in first class. Also, my legs are too long for coach. So really, first class is the only way to fly with me.

Sierra: Twist my arm, why don't you?

Chance: See you at SFO tomorrow. Can't wait.

That's how you treat a fake date. You make sure she travels in style.

* * *

I arrive at the gate early and scan the room for Sierra. As I look for waves of thick blonde hair, high cheekbones, and lush lips, my pulse surges.

A few seconds later, I spot her lounging in a leather chair, looking like she couldn't possibly belong anyplace else but waiting for me in the first-class lounge. My pulse zooms from surge to skyrocket.

Thanks, attraction. This is going to be a hard trip.

There's nothing fake about the way I react to her. But I'm going to have to fake my way through the next forty-eight hours and pretend I don't want to share a room with her, strip her down to nothing, tie her up, pin her down, take her, have her, lavish her in orgasms.

When I reach her, I pull out my cool and calm persona, the one I use on the mound.

"If it isn't the budding Cougars fan," I say.

A smile brightens her face. "Close, but you haven't

convinced me yet, Chance."

"But I will."

And as hard as it may be to fake it with her, hard also feels pretty fucking good.

I haven't felt good with a woman in a long time.

* * *

As the plane fills, the flight attendant brings us mango cocktails. We thank her, then I lift my glass, and Sierra does the same. "Here's to weddings, to dates, and to never letting an ex see you sweat," Sierra says.

I clink my glass to hers. "I'll drink to that."

We each take a sip, then set the glasses down in the console between our cushy leather seats in the second row. This is as good a time as any. I rub my palms together. "We have five hours on the plane. We should get our details straight in case anyone asks . . . so, is this our first date?"

She hums as if considering the question while she twirls the pink-streaked strands in her hair. "I think we probably went on a couple dates in San Francisco, don't you think?"

I nod my approval. "We definitely did. Best dates ever, if memory serves?"

She tosses a sexy grin my way. "Of course they were. We hit it off. In fact, I think you asked me out just maybe a few weeks ago?"

"Damn right I did. It was that night I walked into your bar and ordered a scotch."

"And after that you had the *Wild Chemistry*." She lifts

her drink, knocks back a little more.

I can't stop staring at her lips on the glass. And then directly at her lips when she puts down the cocktail. Those lush pink lips. "And I felt some kind of wild chemistry. That's what inspired me to ask you out that damn night. Something I've been wanting to do for a long time," I say, spinning the tale of our first date that's hardly a fable at all.

"I'd been wanting you to for the longest time," she says, all smoky and sexy and so damn believable.

Why not go for broke? In this fake dating scenario, why shouldn't our backstory be as electric as it could be? I tell the next chapter. "When you said yes, all I could think was—dirty dreams do come true. But we couldn't even really wait for our date, could we?"

She runs her fingertips along her collarbone. "That's right. I left work early. My manager took over."

I pick up the thread and paint the next scene. "I took you to my place," I say, my voice going lower as the temperature in me shoots higher.

She moves a bit closer, parts her lips, takes her time. "You could barely even wait till the door closed."

This paint-by-numbers sex-capade is getting out of hand, and I fucking love it. "I'd only been fantasizing about it for the last year," I say, my husky tone surely giving away my truth. But I'm not sure I care right now about anything but this fake story that feels deliciously real.

"And I was glad you didn't waste any time. There's something so wild about hot, up-against-the-door sex, don't you think?"

Hell fucking yes. "So very hot and electric," I say, wanting to have that with her now.

Tonight.

Tomorrow.

She runs the tip of her tongue along her teeth, licks her lips, then says, "The first of many times. It sure seemed like we couldn't stop once we got started."

"It's a wonder we're not fucking right now," I whisper.

Yep. It's the eighth wonder of the modern sex world.

"Can I interest you in a pineapple macadamia nut salad once we're airborne?"

I blink, reconnecting with reality as I swing my gaze to the cheery, redhead flight attendant asking the question.

"Sure," I say, my voice still a little rough from the dirty flirting.

"And for you?" the woman asks my partner-in-hypothetical-crime.

"Yes, please," Sierra answers, and it sounds like she's having a hard time clearing the fog too.

When the attendant moves on to the next row, my eyes connect with Sierra's again. Hers seem to be flickering with heat. "But, no one's going to be asking us about our fake sex life," she says, with a light laugh.

"Yeah. That'd be way too personal," I say.

She clears her throat. "I think we could just say you asked me out that night, we went out a few times, and we were really into each other."

That feels true enough, but it's nowhere near as enticing.

9

CHANCE

Somewhere over the Pacific, I catch Sierra studying me, her head tilted as if I'm a puzzle, and I pause the movie and pop out my earbud. "What? Do I have pineapple in my beard?"

"No, I was just wondering—at the risk of asking you the question you've been dreading—are you still hung up on Natasha?"

Whoa. That came out of nowhere. "Do I not seem over her? I'm definitely over her."

I'm over her so much I'm way into you, gorgeous.

The pretty blonde lounging by the window levels me with a direct stare. "You did ask me to be your wedding date in case people asked about her. I thought maybe the relationship was still a sore spot, which would be understandable because you were together for a long time." Her voice softens, along with her brown eyes. It's only the two of us in this row, but with her gentle tone and the hum of the plane, it almost feels like we're all alone in the cocoon of this conversation. "And I'm asking you as your friend."

I take a beat, weighing her question. I want to answer her honestly, as a friend, but also as a man who's interested in her.

"I asked you to be my date because I'm definitely over her, but people have a way of *not* believing that. Know what I mean?"

"I do."

"And having you there will help them believe. I'll still answer all the *how are you doing* and *are you okay* questions people will ask because they're concerned. My mom's cousin, and her sisters. And Blake, since he worries about everyone's happiness. My dad might. My mom won't, since she's been endlessly asking me how I'm doing and trusts me when I say I'm good. But she's always been open about it, and we've talked frankly about my split."

"That's good, to be able to talk to her."

"Yeah, she's sort of insistent on talking. It's her thing. Along with people using her first name. So, call her Penny."

Sierra taps her temple. "Noted."

"But as for others . . . eh, I don't want to deal with it. Sort of like when we lost the playoffs, and TJ pretended to be me at The Lucky Spot so I wouldn't have to field the fan sympathy."

She gapes. Her hand flies to her mouth. When she lowers it, she asks in a hushed whisper, "You guys did that?"

I wiggle a brow, playing up my devilish side. "Sometimes, we misbehave badly. It's a twin thing."

"Have you ever done that with dates?"

I meet her gaze dead on. "You do know TJ and I have different tastes? I'm pretty sure you and I have already had that whole *hey, we both like plants, have gay brothers, and enjoy bingeing on British comedies* talk, right?"

She gives me a *duh* look. "Yes, I'm aware we have lots in common, baseball allegiances notwithstanding. But my point is, identical twins can pull off all sorts of shenanigans. And it's not like you or he would be kissing one of your dates. But if you missed a date because of a game, or if he missed one because he was on deadline . . . you could pretend," she suggests with a twinkle in her eyes. A twinkle that does make me wonder if Sierra has a naughty side. One that likes bedroom games.

I go along with the vibe. "I don't mind a little make-believe. Under the right circumstances."

The corner of her lip twitches. "Is that so?"

"I'm pretty open-minded. To all sorts of things." *Like taking you against the wall.*

"Good to know," she says, her voice a little breathy.

"But to answer your question, I never pretended to be TJ on a date or vice versa. But if he ever needed me to dump some dude who'd been a total douche to him, I'd be all over that in a heartbeat."

She laughs lightly. "Okay, it's seriously adorable that you'd do that for him."

"We're pretty tight. He actually offered to play me

this weekend at the wedding if I really wanted to get out of it."

"He did? I love that, how you look out for each other."

"Me too," I say, then I tap her arm. A friendly bit of affection. Well, mostly friendly. "But I'm stoked to be going with you. It'll be a blast. And, yeah, I *also* don't want to be seen as a bridesmaid's ex. I'm in a new era of my life, if you will, and . . ." I stop, breathe out hard, laugh at myself. "Whoa. Did I just sound like a social media douche or what?"

"Like you have an Instagram feed where you spout platitudes about life phases and stuff," she says, laughing.

I drag a hand down my face, making light of it all. "That's it. You can't take me anywhere."

"I'll tell the pilot to turn this jet around. I'll let him know you're retiring from all social interaction. I'm sure he'll understand."

"It's the only recourse for what I just said."

She's quiet for a few seconds, then drums her unpolished nails against the console between us. "Seriously, though, I get it. You want to go as Chance Ashford, not as Chance who was once part of Chance and Natasha. But can I ask you a question?"

"Isn't that kind of what you've been doing all along? Why stop now?"

Sierra takes a deep breath, gearing up for something. "How are you doing, Chance? In all seriousness."

As her brown eyes lock with mine again, the rest of

the plane seems to disappear, like it's just us two in this metal tube traveling across the sky.

Her question is a good one.

How *am* I doing?

At the moment, I'm flying over the ocean in first class with a gorgeous woman I've been insanely interested in for a year—the *only* woman who's caught my eye since I've been single. A woman I want. A woman I can't have, but even so, I'm doing great. "I feel fantastic. Especially right now."

Her eyes sparkle. "Good. That's good."

"And listen," I say, preemptively, since I want to share *this* too. "You know I was married for a while. And yes, you know how it ended. It was public and frustrating, and it sucked like losing the playoffs suck. But the truth is...the end of my marriage didn't surprise me. Was I hurt? Yes. But we'd been growing apart for some time."

"It's sad when that happens." She squeezes my arm and it feels a whole lot of nice having her soft hand on me.

"She wasn't happy with my job and hadn't been for a long time. She didn't care for how often I was gone."

Sierra flinches. "Really? She didn't like the baseball-wife lifestyle?"

"She hated me being on the road. She said I was married to the game."

"Do you think you were?" The question comes out earnestly, not as an accusation. That makes it easy to answer truthfully.

"To some degree, yes. It's hard to compete at the top

level without being married to the sport. So, I probably was. I probably still am. And since Natasha and I were together in college, it's easy to say *that's what she signed up for.* But that's not entirely fair either. At the time we got married, she was fine with it, or said she was. But then she changed, and she wanted different things. She wanted more of me. And I couldn't give that to her."

"Do you wish you'd been able to? Do you regret anything?"

"No, but I believe in quality of time, not quantity. If you devote your whole heart to something, like a romance, you can make it work. You might not be able to see each other every day, but you can talk on the phone, you can text, and you can stay in touch."

"Exactly. You can be close to each other even if you aren't in the same house every second." Her eyes spark with intensity. "Grant is like that with Declan. They're both constantly traveling, as you know, and they don't see each other that often, but they're so connected even when they're apart. Then when they're together, it's . . . magic."

Her smile is fucking magic. A wide, genuine one for her brother.

Grant and his boyfriend are obviously happy. They aren't together too frequently during the season, but when they are, everyone can tell how much they care for each other. "They make the best of it when they're together. Those two guys are couple goals."

"Definitely." Sierra sinks back into the leather chair, like she's basking both in the comfort of the plane and in the happiness her brother has found. "Seeing them together—it makes me feel like anything is possible. They make the best of everything. That's what I would want in a relationship."

Who wouldn't?

Except, not me, and not now.

Too bad it seems Sierra's on a different path at the moment. "You're looking for something serious? Like they have?"

A cough seems to burst from her chest. "No way. Well, not now. Maybe at some point down the road, but at the moment I'm not looking for a relationship *at all.*"

Shut the front door.

All the lights flash bright at once.

The buzzers ring.

Is she saying she wants fun without strings? "You're not looking for a boyfriend?" I ask, full of a new, wild hope.

She scoffs. "I got out of a long-term one a year ago. I'm kind of married to The Spotted Zebra. All I want is to enjoy myself while I can."

And I want to enjoy her. All night long.

"Nothing wrong with that," I say, with a big smile and perhaps a new goal.

For now, I'm just going to let her enticing words —*enjoy myself*—marinate for a little longer in my mind. Figure out what to do with them. That's my new mission for the rest of the day. Understand her even more.

And since we're on the topic of relationships and exes, there's something I've been wondering about. "What about Joe?"

She gives a confused look. "Joe who?"

"Really? That's it? Joe who? Your ex."

"Oh. Him. He's ancient history." She flaps a hand dismissively behind her. "He's eons and eras and entire epochs away."

That's very good to know too. She's not on the rebound. She's just doing what she wants. Like me. The same-page-ness of us makes me very, very happy. "Good. I like that."

She smiles softly. "Me too."

I feel this moment tipping into something more than friends or flirting, imagine the heat turning from simmering to scorching.

But then Sierra yawns, a reminder that the woman needs to relax. "Put your feet up. Lie back. Rest."

"Mmm. That sounds perfect." She lowers the seat, turns her head to the side, and closes her eyes. Then, she stretches her arm lazily across the console, rests her hand on my bicep, and snoozes just like that.

She sleeps the rest of the way to Hawaii, and something about it feels a lot like a real date and only a little like a fake one.

10

SIERRA

We step off the plane as a warm, ocean breeze drifts gently by. Hawaiian music plays overhead in the open walkways of the terminal.

Tropical air warms my skin, and my heart.

We are not in San Francisco anymore, and I love it.

After we grab our luggage, the car Chance ordered arrives at the curb. I give the sleek black vehicle a once-over, adding an appreciative whistle. “Ooh la-la, traveling in style.”

Chance winks. “Told you I’d convince you.”

“That you travel well? Consider me convinced,” I say as the driver hoists our bags into the trunk and Chance thanks him.

“Hey, I want you to be convinced to be a fan too. So consider this part of me being a Cougars ambassador.”

“Well, Mister Ambassador,” I say as I slide into the back seat, “I enjoy first-class travel. A fancy town car with leather seats. I love it.”

Chance gets in next to me. "Good. Because I want my date to enjoy every second of this weekend."

You have no idea how much your date wants to enjoy this weekend.

"I intend to," I say, keeping it light.

We chat about the view and the island as we cruise along the highway, the ocean unfurling as we go. Waves crest as surfers ride them, and families play on the sand.

Everything about this island relaxes me.

It's a far cry from my bar, the chores, and all the things I need to do as I expand. But I don't mind this getaway, and I'm so glad I flew in earlier than planned.

I wish Chance and I were here for real, enjoying each other in every way on this tropical escape, and for a moment, I thought maybe we might have been. Playing sexy make-believe on the plane here was fun.

But when he spoke about Natasha, he reminded me what I really am—his cover, and what we really have—a blossoming friendship that I'm starting to treasure.

At the hotel, my *date* heads to the VIP check-in. I gesture to the regular line. "I should go to the other one. I'm not a VIP."

Chance laughs, tips his forehead toward his line. "Sierra, of course you are."

"I'm not. I just have a regular room."

"It's cool. You're with me. You can check in with the VIP too."

Who am I to turn down his baller lifestyle? I go

along with the man, loving the perks. A few seconds later, a perky Hawaiian woman at the concierge desk calls us over. With crisp efficiency, she checks Chance into the Luau Suite.

"That comes complete with a king-size bed, a mini fridge, a terrace balcony, an ocean view, a living room with a pullout couch, and complimentary coffee, tea, and fruit for breakfast," she says.

He turns to me, gives a shrug. "What can I say? I do like my comforts."

I raise a finger. "Never apologize for that."

"Then I never will."

When it's my turn, I give her my name. "Sierra Blackwood. I just have a regular room."

"Fantastic. I'll check you in too." She taps away on the keyboard, peering intently at the computer screen, her glasses sliding down her nose. "Ohhhh." Her brow knits as she pushes the glasses back up.

"What's wrong?" I ask.

She taps some more. Clears her throat. Looks up from the screen. "I'm so sorry, Ms. Blackwood. It appears there's been a mix-up."

That doesn't sound good. "What sort of mix-up?"

"The extra room. We don't actually have one anymore. It looks like it went back into the room block and was then booked to someone else."

No big deal. That can't be the only room in the hotel. "I'll just take another room. Whatever you have available will be fine."

The woman winces, her kind eyes revealing her disappointment. "That's the issue."

Tension slides down my spine. "What do you mean?"

"I'm so sorry but we're fully booked."

Frustration kicks in. I don't want to search for another hotel. Or hunt for an Airbnb. I just want to get in a hammock and relax.

But I can't.

Chin up, Sierra. Deal like you deal with every little thing at the bar.

"I'll just find another hotel," I say with forced cheer, grabbing my phone from my pocket and tapping away. Chance sets a hand on my arm. "I have a suite. You take the bed. I'll take the pullout couch."

My gaze meets his. His brown eyes are serious, his expression intense. "Let me do this for you. I want to," he adds, brooking no argument.

That's all. No pile of reasons. No long explanations. Just an *I want to.*

And sometimes, that's enough.

Part of me thinks I should decline. Insist on finding another room come hell or high water. Staying with Chance is playing with fire—he's already made it clear that his guy code rules apply to me.

Rules I respect.

But the way he's looking at me makes my heart beat faster. It warms my skin.

And makes me suspect the code might be crumbling a bit for him.

I want to say yes so badly.

So, I do.

11

SIERRA

This is what couples do on honeymoons and romantic getaways.

Walk into a luxurious, sex-drenched suite and gawk at it together.

Just look at that bed.

It's king-size, maybe even bigger. It's more like *fuck me all night long* size and it sports a white, fluffy duvet that makes me want to fall onto it like a naughty angel. To ask him how he thinks I look in burgundy lace, stretched out on this pure white bed.

The whole ensemble screams "take me now."

Right now.

Or maybe that's what my body is saying.

The smells are an aphrodisiac too—gardenia and coconut, pineapple and luxury. Right along with a salty breeze billowing through softly blowing curtains. The sliding glass doors open to a terrace with a spectacular view of the endless ocean.

But the bed keeps pulling my focus.

It has its own heartbeat. It's the pulse of the room. Maybe it even has a voice too, like it's daring us to explore it.

Come lie down . . .

Since the bedroom is not quite a bedroom—it's more like an extension of the living room. I can't shut the door on him tonight and hide out in the bedroom, and nor do I want to.

Especially since the thought of Chance, and his big, long athletic frame trying to fit comfortably on that pullout couch nags at me.

I don't like that image at all.

I want him to feel as good as I bet I'll feel in bed tonight.

Chance sets down his bag on the tiled floor in the living room, then turns to me, a look in his brown eyes that's both inviting and nervous. "So, Sierra? Is this suite better than camping on the beach?"

I drop my bag on the floor, then throw my arms around him impulsively. "You are my hero." I'm so relieved, so grateful. "I didn't want to find another place," I tell him as I bury my face in his neck, inhaling the scent of his woodsy aftershave that's fading as the day goes on.

Still, he smells so damn good.

There's nothing quite like the scent of a man who turns you on.

As I hold him a little more tightly, a gruff noise falls from his throat as he murmurs, "I didn't want you to either."

He loops his strong arms around my waist, tugging me a little closer.

The tropical breeze mingles with his hair. Here in his suite—no, *our* suite—we must seem exactly like a couple on a romantic escape.

We feel like one to me.

Maybe to him too?

His hand rubs gently against the small of my back. He murmurs as he brings me close. Perhaps this isn't fake for him at all.

Nothing feels like pretend, and neither one of us is breaking this embrace that's zoomed well past friendly. This hug is living firmly in prelude-to-more land, complete with roaming palms and deep, sexy sighs.

I flash back to my *Wild Chemistry* drink. To all my reasons for concocting it—to lay my wishes on the line with Chance.

I didn't that night, of course.

But now sure as hell feels like the moment to voice my request.

The pull between us feels completely mutual.

And totally inescapable.

The intensity of this newfound awareness is like a low, steady drumbeat that soundtracks my desire.

A desire that's growing stronger by the minute.

Maybe this is the time to serve up the metaphorical drink and extend an invitation to get in my pants.

I break the embrace, curling a hand over his shoulder. "So, Chance . . ."

"Yes?"

The heat in his eyes tells me to go for it, but there's a

flicker of nerves there too. Maybe some understandable reservations.

Before I can jump in and tell him all the things I'd like for him to do to me tonight, the planner in me shoves the impulsive part clear out of the way.

I need to get my bearings. I know what I want, but this man has a code. I've waited this long. I can wait a little longer to make sure he's truly ready to break his rules.

Chance works with my brother, and I don't want to mess things up for either one of them.

Sex can ruin a friendship—any relationship, really. It can derail your whole damn future.

Best to be certain.

I put on my best *everything is cool* face, tipping my head to indicate the rest of the suite. "Do you want to explore?" I ask, as if that's what I meant to say all along.

"Let's do it," he says.

As we check out the suite, he walks past the bed, pats it, and says, "You'll sleep so damn soundly tonight."

Impulsive me wants to add, "And there's enough room for you to sleep next to me," but his phone buzzes.

That's a relief for planner me.

Chance grabs it from his pocket, slides open the screen, then says, "It's TJ. He says the party's going to start in about an hour."

I look at my attire, wrinkled from the plane. I glance in the nearby mirror. My hair needs some va-va-voom. My face needs a freshening up. Saved by circumstance. "I should . . . shower."

Chance looks down at himself, backs up. "Same."

I am dying to say *shower with me.*

Instead, I purse my lips so I don't blurt out that tantalizing invitation.

I'm so damn good at holding in my desires.

He clears his throat. "Why don't you take the first shower?"

"Good idea." I grab my toiletries from my bag, some fresh lingerie, and a sundress, then head into the bathroom, shutting the door.

I sink against it.

What the hell am I supposed to do?

My pulse races. My face is flush. And my panties are soaked.

I have no clue how I'm going to survive being near the man I madly crave.

A few deep breaths.

I try to center myself, fanning my face to cool down.

Then I pull myself away from the door.

I don't lock it, though. Chance is a gentleman and I know he won't come in, but there's something so deliciously naughty about the idea that he could.

And I like naughty.

I'd like to invite it into my life this weekend.

But now isn't that time.

12

CHANCE

The shower beats a tantalizing rhythm of desire.

I make my way to the balcony, curling my hands over the railing, gripping it tightly.

Holding on takes sheer iron will.

I want to head into the bathroom, open the door, shed all my clothes, step inside the shower. Kiss the breath out of her as hot water pours over both of us.

Instead, I white-knuckle it through the next few minutes, staring at the ocean, trying desperately to key in on anything but the images racing through my head.

Water sliding over her lush body. Soap glistening on her skin, her hands in her hair as she tips her head back under the stream.

I grip harder. It's a wonder I don't break this railing.

These two nights are going to be torture.

But I want the torture. The torture makes me feel wildly alive. I haven't felt like this in ages, and the rush of lust is incredible. The only thing that comes close is striding across the field, taking the mound in the bottom of the ninth with the bases loaded.

The moment when I'm the one thing that stands between the other team winning or losing.

I get that same wild thrill as I imagine all these filthy possibilities with Sierra Blackwood.

Ten minutes later, she emerges from the bathroom. I turn around as she makes her way to the terrace, stops in the doorway.

A dark pink sundress hugs her breasts, then falls softly down her body, flaring out from her waist, stopping at her knees. Purple and red flowers twist in a pattern across the fabric. Cherry blossom ink dances down her arm, looking brighter post-shower. Or maybe it's my imagination. Maybe everything about her is turned up several degrees. Her hair is still wet and impossibly sexy. She holds a hairdryer.

I can barely breathe. But breathing is overrated when I'm near her.

I can't mince words. I can't fucking fake a thing now. I scrub a hand down my face as I say, "Wow. You look . . . incredible."

She smiles, soft and inviting. "Thank you. I'm glad you like your *date.*" The words come out more sensually than before.

A groan escapes my lips. "I like my date a lot," I say in a rough whisper.

I like her so much I have to walk right past her, fists clenched, and head to the bathroom before I do something dangerous.

Like draw her in close and plant a hot, scorching kiss on those lips.

I lock the bathroom door behind me and seriously consider whacking off as I turn on the shower.

Between the steam enrobing the room, the scent of berry lingering from her body wash, and the smell of her that's every-fucking-where, I'd go from zero to blast off in under two minutes, no doubt.

But I've got to get these feelings under control.

And I *have* control.

That's what makes me millions of dollars a year. I have so much fucking control and I need it to get a handle on tonight.

Or . . . do I?

My mind flicks back to her comments on the plane.

She's not interested in a relationship.

She doesn't want to get serious.

Maybe tonight, we can bend the golden rule.

I've been refusing to think of her sexually—well, more than I already do—because I don't want a messy entanglement with a teammate's sister. But if she doesn't want to get serious, then that rule doesn't apply.

Especially when two adults might want the same damn thing—for dirty dreams to come true, like we said on the plane.

This wedding date started as a show-the-world-you're-a-good-sport plan. Maybe it's still that. But what if it's a two-way road, and we're headed to the same place?

The bedroom.

My new agenda for tonight? Find the fuck out.

* * *

Island music floats through the open door as the sun dips toward the edge of the ocean.

Sierra gazes at the sea, resting on her elbows.

Her hair is dry now, curling softly over her shoulders, and she's still barefoot. As I walk through the living room, past the coffee table with the hairdryer on it, I catch a glimpse of a pink cotton bra strap peeking out from the strap of her sundress.

I rein in a groan of desire when I join her on the terrace. As she removes her AirPods, she takes in my attire with an approving nod at my blue linen shirt and khaki shorts. "You're looking good."

"I'm a fashion rock star." I nod to her phone. "Listening to anything interesting?"

"Rearranging Your Sock Drawer in Five Simple Steps," she deadpans.

"Excellent. Next we'll have you listening to How to Organize your Utensils."

"I've got that queued up and ready to go." As she tucks her phone and AirPods into her purse, she says, "Actually, I was listening to Lulu Rhodes. This female comic I found. She talks about the challenges of dating and adulting. Very self-deprecating. I'm actually thinking of expanding The Spotted Zebra and having stand-up comedy once a week. Some of my favorite lady comics."

"That's fantastic. Save me a seat in the front row at your comedy nights," I say, flashing forward to life back in San Francisco. If we indulged in a fling here, would I still be able to go to her bar with the guys next season after games? To her comedy nights? Hell yeah. We're both adults. We could handle that. "How is it going, finding the talent?" I ask.

"My friends and I are on the hunt. Clementine, Trish, Erin, and I like to check out clubs in the city and see some of the women," Sierra says as she brushes some hair off her shoulder. "Plus, after I return from this wedding, I'm going to Vegas for two days to check out Lulu in person and also a bartender who supposedly makes both amazing drinks and does those fantastic bar tricks." She mimes flipping a cocktail bottle.

"Two trips in a row," I say. "I'd say you're taking relaxing seriously, but it sounds like you're still as relentless as ever."

"Relentless is my middle name." Sierra picks up her purse. "So, this whole fake date thing. Part of the plan was we need a picture, right?"

It sure was. But I didn't script the photo or plan the caption in advance. Now that we're doing it, questions flash before me.

How far are we pushing this fake date narrative online? What do I call her on social? Do I make sure we look . . . affectionate?

"So, I just post a pic of us and say you're my date? Confession: I'm not a pro at dating. Or posting personal stuff online."

She touches my biceps, her hand nice and soft. "I'm not either. But my friends are great at the whole live-my-life-online, so we just keep it simple and fun."

That's the order of this fake date business.

And we should do it now to get out in front of this pretend fling. If we don't, a guest at the hotel could recognize me and post something. If I've learned anything from Natasha's online persona, it's that nothing stays private for long.

I'm here with a brilliant, successful, passionate, badass babe and I don't mind showing her off. I fish my phone from my pocket, and we line up by the terrace. I slide in next to her. She inches closer, and yeah, that's another clue—the way she presses her body right next to me. Then, she lets loose a soft, low hum.

I stretch out my arm and snap a selfie of us.

Not a single thing about this picture feels fake at all.

When I check the image of her curled up by my side, looking both sweet and sexy, it sure as hell seems like we're on a date.

Feels like we are too.

I write up a draft and show her the caption: *Not a bad start to the off-season. Hawaii, pre-wedding party with my gorgeous, brilliant date—life is good.*

I'm no wordsmith like my brother, but this feels just right. Hope she thinks so too.

"Ohhh," Sierra says in a purr as she reads. "Flattery is the way to my heart."

I level her with a stare, then swallow roughly. "It's not flattery. It's all true," I say.

Her eyes stay locked on mine. She nibbles the corner of her lips. "Good," she whispers. "Same."

And the answer to whether Sierra wants to level up seems to be *yes.*

"And here's my confession," she says, glancing

around the suite. "Thank you for insisting I stay with you. I kind of can't wait to go to bed tonight."

I stifle a cough. The thought of her in bed is going to be the death of my control.

"Let's get you away from that temptation right now," I say.

But maybe later we can give in. All the way.

I'm pretty sure I won't even have to throw out my good-guy card if we do.

Since these vibes I'm getting from her—the long embrace and the lingering gazes—are telling me to go ahead and exercise that loophole.

13

CHANCE

As we walk through the hotel, possibilities for tonight unfold in my mind.

After the party. Coming together. Crashing into each other.

That moment when you both look at each other and you just know that all the tension between the two of you is about to snap in the most delicious way.

I can't wait.

But I have to, so we chat about surfing—she wants to go, I'm prohibited by my contract—as we cross along the pool to the garden area, filled with tables and servers and family members. As we walk over the grass, I reach for her hand, thread my fingers through hers, and squeeze.

Sierra smiles, and as we hold hands, the temptation intensifies.

The only thing saving me from acting on it is that we're here at the rehearsal party.

And it's a crush of people.

Including my mom.

When her gaze catches mine, she rushes past palm trees and picnic tables to toss her arms around me. "My baby boy. I haven't seen you in ages."

"Hmm. Then was it my other mother I saw last month right before the playoff game we lost?" I ask, teasing her when I disentangle myself.

Mom peers at me through her cherry-red glasses. "Well, it feels like ages. That's just how it goes for a mom. Also, next year, your team needs to remember to hit the ball, dear. I've told you that. You can't record those saves if there's nothing to save."

I laugh. "I know. Trust me, I know."

She pats my head, something she's good at since TJ and I got our height from her—she's six feet tall, and our dad is two inches shorter.

"Want me to remind them?" Mom says it playfully, but the truth is, she'd do it—issue orders to the Cougars lineup. Mom is a fixer—she runs a business consultancy and tells other businesses how to fix their shit. She's just that way.

She was direct with us growing up. She didn't tell TJ his stories were perfect—she challenged him to make every word better. Same for me with baseball. She rooted for me every step of the way, and also urged me to improve when I needed to, to give it my all when I wasn't doing that.

She's a straight shooter, and I always know where I stand with her.

Mom smiles, swings her gaze to Sierra. "Hello there.

You must be Sierra. I love your ink. And your little pink streak."

"Thank you so much," Sierra says, patting her hair. "Pleasure to meet you . . . Penny."

Mom's green eyes twinkle as they snap to me. "Well done, Chance."

"You only beat it into my head a million times . . . *Penny*."

Mom waves a dismissive hand at me as she addresses Sierra. "My sons are full of sass, especially this one. Now, are you liking Hawaii? Did you know there are sea turtles right along the edge of the property?"

"I didn't but I'd love to see them."

"I'll show you," she says, and tugs my date away from the crowd. And I already miss her.

A hand comes down on my shoulder. "Shocking. Mom making friends with people right away."

It's TJ.

I turn to my brother, then heave an aggrieved sigh, flapping my hand at his get-up. Shorts and a blue shirt. "Are you kidding me? You're wearing the same color. We look like fucking twins."

His eyebrows wiggle. "Newsflash—we are. Also, I hate to break it to you, but these are not even remotely the same color." He wags a finger at his shirt, then at mine. "You're wearing a sky blue, solid color shirt, and it fits like a sack. Translation—*boring*." He plucks at his shirt. "This is teal and it's form-fitting." He shakes his head like he can't believe my fashion mistake. "Plus, do you not see the tiny mini skulls with daisies in the eyes? My shirt has a badass pattern."

I hold up my hands in surrender. "I can't keep up with you and your clothes."

TJ eyes me up and down dubiously. "I gathered that. Just remember this—I'm the height of understated, thrifted, fashion fun. It's a thing. You, baby boy, are . . . Target. Just Target."

"I like Target."

"That's coming through loud and clear. But hey, it works for you. Just didn't want you to worry we look alike, because I assure you, we do not."

"I'll trust you on this."

"Yes. Yes, you will." TJ tips his gaze to Mom, pointing out sea turtles as she walks along the grounds with Sierra. "What's the story? Is this a real date now? It was fake when we last talked, but seeing you together makes me think you leveled up. You looked cozy."

I breathe heavily, pinch the bridge of my nose, try to sort through the zing of emotion and sensation. "It felt cozy to me too."

TJ has always understood relationship nuances and complexities. They're his stock and trade. He's exactly who I need to talk to right now.

I scrub a hand across my beard and motion for him to step a few feet away from the crowd, where Hawaiian music plays softly from the speakers on the ground.

"Can I ask you a question?" I ask quietly.

"Can I stop you?" TJ jokes, then turns serious. "You know you can. Anytime."

I've mostly worked this out for myself, but if I'm going to step over a big, fat line, I want a second opinion. Validation that I'm doing the right thing, or least not doing a wrong one. "Am I breaking the rule if she's not interested in a relationship either?"

His brow knits. "Which rule?"

"The 'Don't hook up with a teammate's sister' rule."

"That's a thing?" he asks, confusion knitting his brow.

"It's the ballplayer's bro code. If you fall for a teammate's sister, you damn well better want to put a ring on it . . . They're like best-friend's sisters, or the coach's daughter—off-limits unless you're serious. Unless they're women you bring home to mom."

TJ clears his throat, then subtly points to Mom and Sierra. "Mom, as in, the person Sierra is talking to right now?"

I shoot him a look. "You know what I mean."

He nods, indicating he does. "I do, but does Grant give a shit about those rules?"

Good question. Grant is very much a live-free-and-be-happy kind of guy. Hell, he's probably happier than he's ever been over in Kauai right now with Declan. "He's very protective of the ladies in his life. He doesn't want to see them with guys who'll break their hearts. But regardless, *I* care about the rules. I don't want to rock the boat at all. So I want to make sure I'm not doing something stupid."

"This is like your pre-ward thing! It's a pre-check. No, wait, you're getting pre-approval for a sex procedure from your insurance company, aka your brother, fount of wisdom on all life issues," he says.

I roll my eyes. "Let's hope it doesn't *feel* like a procedure. *If* we do that."

"I'll drink to that," he says, lifting an imaginary glass. "May sex be spontaneous, passionate and procedure-free." TJ wraps an arm around my shoulders. "But seriously, Chance, you like to make sure everyone's going to be okay before you do something. You've always wanted everyone to be happy. That's how you were when Mom and Dad got divorced—making sure Mom was happy, that Dad was doing okay."

I flash back to age fourteen, to the night they told us. They were straightforward, open and supportive of each other. The epitome of an *amicable divorce.*

"Yes, that sounds like me," I admit with a shrug. "But weren't you like that then? Wanting to make sure everyone was all good?"

TJ scoffs. "No. I was too caught up in what was happening to me. Maybe that makes me selfish, but it's true."

"I never once thought you were selfish," I tell him.

TJ came out to me when we were fifteen. We were on the hunt for a new burger joint in the Capitol Hill neighborhood of Seattle, our hometown. As we walked, his gaze strayed to a guy maybe a year or two older than us.

"You know him?" I asked.

TJ shook his head. He met my eyes for a weighty beat, then said, "No, but I want to."

"Oh," I said as I processed his meaning. I was only taken aback for the briefest moment, maybe because of the ease with which he'd said it. "You think he's cute?"

TJ gave a small smile, a little embarrassed. "I do."

"That's cool," I said, smiling too. I was psyched for

him, that he knew who he was and what he wanted. "Does anyone else know?"

"You're the first person I've told." He blew out a long, relieved breath. "I've been wanting to tell you for so long."

I was grateful to be trusted. "I'm glad you said it, and I'm glad you told me." Then I stopped walking and dragged him in for a hug. When I let go, I asked, "Will you tell Mom and Dad soon?"

"Definitely." He swallowed, looking a little nervous. "I'd appreciate it if you were there. Will you be?"

I clapped his back, reassuring him, happy that we had this kind of relationship. Teachers, coaches, and friends have always been fascinated by our twin connection—do we have twin telepathy? A special bond where we feel each other's pain or joy?

Nah.

Nothing like that. We *do* have a deep bond, but I don't think it's a twin thing. We're connected because we give a shit about each other.

I shake off the memory, returning to here and now. "But do you think I just want people to get along? And that I'm doing that here—smoothing the way before I pursue what I want?"

TJ gives a sharp nod. "You want others around you to be good with your choices. Dad's the same. I mean, c'mon, even when they divorced, he tried to do the whole co-living thing. He wanted Mom to like him even as his ex. That's just his thing."

A dentist with a pediatric practice, our father's job is literally to win over people who want to run from him.

Maybe I've always been trying to be like him—the guy who can hold it together for everyone.

But is that who I want to be?

Or do I want to be the man who walks up to Sierra Blackwood, spins her around, and tells her I'm dying to spend the night with her? We're both adults. We don't need to be in love. We don't need to be anything. We can just . . . be.

"Should I—"

But before I can finish the question, I spot Blake, all broad shoulders and wide grin. He closes the distance to us in seconds, brings TJ and I both in for a hug. "My favorite cousins," he says, then lets us go. "Can you believe it? I'm getting hitched. Me! The guy who was terrified to ask a girl to the high school prom."

"Pretty sure we were all terrified of that," I say.

"Seconded," TJ says. Then he pats our cousin's chest. "But you have come into your own, Blake. Happy for you."

"So happy you'll buy a hot tub?" Blake asks playfully.

I roll my eyes. "This again, Hot Tub King?"

Blake holds out his hands wide. "C'mon. I'm a salesman. I can't *not* try to get you to buy a hot tub of love."

"You're hardly the salesman," I point out as I scratch my head. "More like, gee, what's it called? The CEO of A Hot Tub for Everyone."

"It's my motto and my mission. Hot tubs are like a lubricant for love. You guys both need them," Blake says. "I'm like a love salesman."

"Sorry, Mr. Love Salesman, I don't have room for

hot tubs or love in my one-bedroom in Chelsea," TJ says, not sounding a bit sorry.

"Someday you will." Blake laughs, then turns to me, his twinkle disappearing, replaced with concern. "Enough about bubbles. How the hell are you doing, Chance? Is it hard being here? I made sure you're not at *her* table."

And here we go.

Dread tightens my neck and shoulders . . . but then I let it go. Who cares about Natasha?

TJ clears his throat, points subtly at our mom, next to Sierra. "Blake, my little bro is here with Trish's friend Sierra. Just make sure Chance is next to the gorgeous, friendly, badass babe he brought with him. Can you do that?"

Yup. This is the twin connection—looking out for each other.

Blake beams. "I can do that." He raps his knuckles on my sternum. "And you're next, Chance. You better be next. And then you," he says to TJ. "And then everyone!" The Hot Tub King raises his arms with this royal decree, then spots someone in the distance and waves. "I gotta chat with Marie and Stephanie."

He takes off, and when he's out of earshot, TJ laughs. "He's not even married yet and he's preaching the gospel of love."

"He's high on life," I say, my eyes returning to Sierra.

As I drink in the view, all thoughts of others fade away.

I feel good.

So damn good that I don't push TJ again for his

opinion. I don't need to double-check the decision. I know what I want—to explore this loophole tonight with my date, and I'm pretty sure she does too.

We won't rock the boat either.

We'll rock the bed instead.

Can it be the end of the party now, please?

TJ nudges me. "I'm going to catch up with Dad. You good?"

"Very good," I say as I stare lustfully at Sierra, enjoying the sight of her silhouetted against the Pacific Ocean, her dress blowing gently around her legs, her hair swishing in the light wind.

Then I spot a flash of scarlet, an alert that the redhead I used to call my wife is striding in my direction.

I wait for annoyance to kick in.

Frustration.

Something.

But it turns out . . . I feel nothing, even when I see sympathy and purpose in Natasha's green eyes.

She stops in front of me. "Hello, Chance. You look . . . well."

"Yeah? I feel well," I tell her, and it's the goddamn truth.

And it has everything to do with someone very much not-her.

She cocks her head, wearing her concern written large on her features. She's "Notes to Self" Natasha through and through as she says, "Glad to hear. But are you sure? You seem distracted."

She probably thinks this is about her. But I don't care. "I'm great," I say.

Then an arm wraps around my waist, a gorgeous body presses to mine, and I feel Sierra's soft lips on my cheek, catch a whiff of her blackberry scent.

It drives me wild.

Natasha's eyes pop to saucer size.

But I don't care one bit about my ex or her reaction. I'm indulging in the attention from Sierra and the soft, sweet feel of her close to me.

I only care about the rightness of this moment.

"Hey, gorgeous," I say to her. Then to Natasha, I add, "This is Sierra. My date." Sierra waggles her fingertips, says hello, then brushes a sexy, seductive kiss along my jawline.

She lingers, then murmurs against my face.

And right then and there, I have the final clue to the puzzle.

Neither one of us believes that this date is fake.

14

SIERRA

His hands pretty much stay on me for the next few hours.

My waist, my hip, my arm.

Chance barely disconnects from me during the pre-wedding party, as waiters and waitresses serve tapas and appetizers to guests in the garden area. He keeps me close, going into full-on *you're my date* mode as we chat with friends like Trish and Clementine, and family too, like TJ and Chance's dad.

That seems to be evidence enough that he's tipping into fuck-the-code territory.

I savor every second of his touch, but I also want to speed up time.

To find out what happens when the door to the Luau Suite closes behind us in a few hours.

If this spark will combust into a fire.

Because that's all we're doing—sparking.

After we nibble on watermelon cubes topped with

feta, he brushes my hair from my shoulder. "So, is your weekend getaway living up to your expectations?"

"It's exceeding them," I say.

And you're exceeding them too.

"Does this mean you're convinced?"

"Oh, was this part of your Cougars campaign?" I toss out.

"Maybe it was." He wiggles a brow and drops a kiss to my cheek. A tingle spreads down my chest, and my eyes flutter closed.

When I open them, I meet his fiery gaze. I lower my voice to a bare whisper. "You're awfully good at this pretend date thing," I murmur.

His lips curve into a sexy grin. "So are you."

It's not pretend for me.

It's not for him either.

In my head, I practice the words I'll say to him when we reach the room.

* * *

A little later, waiters circulate with trays of chocolate-covered strawberries and mini coconut cakes.

Chance darts out a hand, grabs a couple strawberries. "My favorite," he says sheepishly.

"Want me to grab some extras just for you? I'll pretend they're for me," I tease.

"Would you?"

Laughing, I oblige, setting the treats on a small plate I'm holding. "You have a chocolate-covered strawberry fetish?"

He bites into one, moans lasciviously. When he's done with the fruit, he nods. "Yes. And I need you to snag as many as possible so I can have them tomorrow for breakfast."

"I'm on it. Just call me a strawberry thief."

"You're a goddess," he says, then devours another one.

I laugh as he moans around the food.

"You're mocking me," he says.

I shrug. "Well, you're kind of making love to a strawberry."

"Mmm. I am shameless. Here. Try one." He holds it out, and I nibble on the end. The juices spread on my tongue, joined by sinfully rich chocolate.

"Fine. It's thievery-worthy," I say.

Chance raises a hand, gently moves it toward my face, then swipes his thumb across my lower lip.

I shiver.

His eyes glitter with lust. "You had a little chocolate," he says, raspy.

"Thanks. I guess they're my downfall too, it seems," I say, but truly, this man might be mine.

Blake clinks his glass. The moment shatters. He's standing at the edge of the garden area, and when he clears his throat, all eyes turn to him.

"Thank you everyone. I just want to say—" The groom stops. Chokes up.

Chance dips his face near my ear, his stubbly jaw coasting along my cheek. "He's a big old teddy bear."

"I figured that out," I say, then Chance slides his arm

around my shoulder, his fingertips tracing the cherries on my ink.

I tremble. Don't even try to hide it anymore.

He's got to notice it.

He's got to be feeling the same thing. Still, I want to know what changed for him since the night he asked me to be his fake date.

Why he seems willing to tango suddenly.

The bro code doesn't seem to matter to this man tonight, and I couldn't be happier. But I do want to know why. I don't want him to have regrets if we sleep together.

Blake draws a deep breath, then tries again. "Thank you so much for coming. Nothing makes me happier than to celebrate the love of my life with all of my friends."

The groom lifts his glass to toast, and the guests give a *cheers,* then a big bear of a man wobbles next to Blake, clasps his shoulder, then shouts happily, "And nothing could make me happier than to be by my brother's side. Except a new hot tub! Hot tubs make me happy! A hot tub for everyone!"

Chance groans.

I wince.

My date dips his mouth near my ear. "And he's probably only had one or two drinks. Jordy gets sloshed after one glass."

Several minutes later as the guests finish with dessert, Jordy weaves across the grass, laughing loudly, spilling a pineapple daiquiri. Chance shoots me an apologetic frown. "I should get him back to his room."

"Of course," I say with false cheer.

Sure, I'm happy that Jordy is getting an escort.

But I was hoping Chance and I would be heading back together.

Instead, after I say goodbye to Clementine, Trish, Penny, and TJ, I head through the hotel alone, down the hall to our suite.

I slide the key in, open the door, close it.

Sigh.

All the flirting on the terrace and the moments at the party had me hoping we'd stumble in together and Chance would push me against the wall.

Slam his body to mine.

Take me hard.

Then I'd tell him I want him to take my V-card, rip it the fuck up, and throw me down on the bed.

I shake my head, trying to shake off this disappointment.

He's helping a family member. I need to stop thinking of only my libido.

I set down my purse and phone on the nightstand, kick off my shoes, and head to the bathroom to get ready for bed.

When I've changed my panties and pulled on a white cotton camisole, he's still not here.

I slide into bed and turn off the light.

* * *

The door jolts open.

I flip to my side, blink, yawn. The clock reads eleven. I've been asleep for . . . twenty minutes.

Chance takes off his shoes, then pads quietly to the bathroom, clearly trying not to wake me.

When he exits a minute later, he's unbuttoning his shirt. I sit up in bed, wide awake now, eager to see him. Ready to tell him. "Hey."

He jerks his gaze to me as he reaches the last button. Damn, the man looks handsome in the dark with the moonlight casting shadows across his face. "I didn't realize you were awake."

"I am. Is Jordy okay?"

Chance seesaws his hand. "He will be. TJ helped me get him to his room, and then he collapsed while singing 'Rolling in the Deep.'"

I tilt my head. "He doesn't strike me as an Adele fan."

"She's mega popular, Sierra," he says.

"I love her," I say, then I draw a deep breath, take an imaginary shot of liquid courage, and say, "But I don't want to talk about music."

Worry etches his brow. "What do you want to talk about?"

There's no time like the present. I'm ready. He's eager. Time to jump. Even as nerves wing through me, so does excitement. "Chance?"

"Yes?"

I push the covers down a little bit, an invitation. "I don't think you should sleep on the couch."

Chance says nothing for the longest time. Just stares at me with desire in his gaze.

"I don't think I should either." He closes the distance, takes off his shirt, strips out of his shorts, and gets into bed with me.

15

CHANCE

There is a time for talking.

And a time for doing.

Sure, we should chat about what this means, what changed, and all that jazz.

But I don't need to dissect any sort of agenda this second.

I've been invited to the only place I want to be.

With her.

So as I slide under the covers, my hand coasts along her hip.

Such a sensual creature, Sierra arches as I trace the curves and dips of her gorgeous body. "You sure don't feel like a fake date, Sierra," I murmur, my fingers delighting in the silk of her skin.

She moves with me, shifting slightly to her side, her brown eyes shimmering. "I don't feel like playing make-believe anymore," she says.

"Me neither." My hand glides across her stomach, so

soft and enticing to the touch. I could worship this stomach. With my lips. My hands. My tongue.

I dip my face to her belly, push up the cotton of her camisole, and press a kiss to her skin, moaning as I inhale her.

She lets out the most fantastic whimper in the world. "Oh God, that feels good."

Her words embolden me. I kiss my way up her stomach, pleasure jolting through my body as my lips travel along her warm skin, landing right under her breasts.

I look up. I fully intend to ravage these beauties.

But it would be rude not to taste her lips first. I move, shifting my weight so that I'm still on my side but my chest covers her, my forearms braced on either side of her body.

She loops her hands around my head, threads her fingers into my hair, and stares into my eyes. "Do you have any idea how long I've wanted to kiss you?"

Pride suffuses me. I grin. "No idea. Why don't you tell me?" I brush my lips across her collarbone, my eyes falling shut from the heady taste of her skin. So sexy and feminine and tropical—she makes my mouth water and my dick throb.

Sierra runs her fingers through my hair, then lifts my face. "Chance, I've been thinking about doing this for a long time. Been thinking about kissing you. Getting you naked." She takes a beat. Swallows. "And asking you something."

My chest heats like the sun. My God, is there

anything hotter than when a woman tells you what she wants?

"Ask me anything," I rasp out as my lips travel along her jawline. It's impossible not to touch her.

Her breath catches as I go, but then she pushes up higher in bed, scooting away from me.

This seems a little serious. I sit too, focus on her mood completely. "You okay? Is anything wrong?"

"I'm great," she says, then exhales. "But I just want to know what changed for you, Chance. From the night you invited me. I don't want you to regret anything. What about your code?"

And maybe we do need to talk after all. She's right to take a breather. "I swear I won't regret a second of this," I say.

"But why? What's different?"

I give her nothing but the truth. "You seem to feel the same way I do."

"You mean since neither one of us wants a relationship?"

"Yes. I'm not interested in one and you said you aren't either. And you and me, we seem to have some kind of crazy chemistry."

"Wild chemistry, I call it," she says with a grin.

"Like your drink," I add.

"Exactly. I made it for you. Because I want you. So much."

"This is officially the sexiest night of my life," I declare. "And I am putting in my order for that drink when we return."

She laughs, then turns a touch serious once more. "So you can break the code if we're having a fling?"

I shrug, adding a smile. "Seems like a good reason to bend it. I'm so into you, Sierra. I want to make you feel incredible in bed."

Humming, she shoots me a flirty grin. "Want to know what I want?"

"I really fucking do."

"Your honesty. Your body. Your straightforward interest in me. No strings attached."

Have I died and gone to dirty heaven?

I believe I have.

"Yes, to all of the above," I say as my hand coasts along her side, over the fabric of her cami and down to the curves of her waist. My whole body vibrates with the need to touch her everywhere. And if she wants honesty, she'll get it. "Sierra, I wanted you the night I walked into the bar and asked you to come here with me. I wanted you the night I walked you home. I've been wanting you for months. And I've been resisting you. And I don't want to resist you any longer."

She shudders, a sensual full-body tremble. "Don't resist me. Chance, I want to sleep with you tonight. And I don't want you to be gentle with me."

A naughty grin curves my lips as I brush my fingers through her hair. "So you like it a little rough?"

She nods, naughty glee in her eyes. "I think so."

"You like it a little hard? A little dirty?"

Her breath comes in a harsh pant. "I do. I don't want to be treated like a flower. I want to be treated like a woman. Like a woman who's not breakable."

I haven't had sex like that in ages. Passionate, can't-get-enough-of-each-other, clawing-at-the-sheets sex. And I want it with Sierra.

A groan works its way up my chest as I drag a hand through her hair. I give a quick tug to test her limits. She gasps, shuddering.

I groan. "You came to the right man. I have only one mission in bed."

"What's that?"

I slide my hands down her body, journeying to her breasts, and I squeeze those beauties too.

She arches her back, her lips parting in an "Oh, *yes . . .*"

"To give you orgasm after orgasm. For you to be drenched in pleasure. For you to come so beautifully hard that you can't form words." I bend my face to her neck, lick the hollow of her throat. "Because you're the woman I can't get out of my mind."

She wraps her hands around my head, drags me closer so her lips are millimeters from mine. The air around us crackles as she whispers in a seductive voice, "Kiss me hard. Make it ruthless."

What the lady wants . . .

I drop my lips to hers, and my body ignites.

It's been years since I felt anything electric. Since I felt passion and heat.

Lust and desire.

And reckless need.

The second our lips connect, I feel all that, all the way down to my toes. I feel it in the pit of my stomach, coiling with need. The desire to touch her everywhere and to give her everything intensifies.

I'm dying to make her feel good and to feel good in return.

I kiss her hard, a deep, long kiss. Sucking on her bottom lip, I tug it between my teeth and yank her closer. There is nothing delicate about our kiss. It's all fire and possession. And the way she claws at my shoulders, jerking me nearer, greedily asking for more, more, more, is all I need to know.

We are so much on the same page with everything.

Fiercely, I claim her mouth, making sure that my beard leaves marks across her skin. She seems to devour my kisses, to hungrily lap them up as she whimpers and moans. I move on top of her, pressing the full length of my body over hers, letting her feel the weight of me, the length of me.

That's what she seems to want. And she takes that as I give it to her. She parts her legs, urging me to press and grind against her panties.

In my boxer briefs, I rock and thrust. She arches and moans. My head swims with lust and my body thrums with the promise of so much passion.

Her hands press against my chest, then she pushes me up. "Chance, I need you to know something," she says, breathy, but there are no nerves in her tone. Just determination in her eyes.

"What is it, gorgeous?"

"I've never had sex before," she says, direct and confident. "And for the longest time I've been wanting you to be the first man to fuck me."

The world slows.

I need a few seconds to process what she's said.

She's a virgin.

But that's all it takes.

I don't need any more time since there is nothing uncertain about Sierra Blackwood's intensity. There's nothing unclear about her statement or her heated gaze.

And when the woman you want asks you to fuck her hard and good, what other answer is there?

I coast a hand down her body. "I would love to fuck you hard and good all night long, gorgeous." Then I dip my face to her neck, sucking hard, making her moan before I let go.

She rocks up against me. "Well, you can start by getting me naked."

16

SIERRA

Finally.

I'm a horse at the races, raring to go.

But seriously?

After all these years, after all these nights, after all my planning,

I'm wearing freaking white.

The utter irony.

I wanted black lace. Pink satin. Or a sexy red teddy. Something hot and fiery to match my desire.

I certainly don't feel virginal.

Wildly curious is more like it.

And yet, I'm in white cotton panties and a cami. The color of innocence.

But then, as I gaze down at my erect nipples poking through the fabric, my panties already soaked, perhaps white is insanely sexy.

Since it reveals all my desire for this man.

A man who gazes at me like he plans to ravage me all night long.

Except . . . his expression shifts.

Uh-oh. Why does he look like someone told him he could never have chocolate-covered strawberries again in his life?

His brow pinches. "I don't have a condom, Sierra. But I'll go to the concierge right now and get one," he says, sliding to the edge of the bed at Mach speed.

I grab his arm right as he reaches for his shorts, stopping him. "I've been wanting to sleep with you for a year, Chance Ashford. I am one hundred percent prepared," I say, like a woman in charge of her pleasure.

He growls. It's the hottest sound I've ever heard.

"I've got everything we need," I add. "I brought a bunch, in fact."

Chance breathes out hard, shuddering. "That is the sexiest thing any woman has ever said to a man in the history of the universe."

With wicked glee rushing through my veins, I hop out of bed, grab my purse, and return with it in a second. I unzip it with excited fingers. Maybe too excited. As I root around in the inside pocket, I miss the condom I'm aiming for. I laugh, embarrassed. "I guess I'm a little nervous," I admit.

Moving behind me on the mattress, he dips his face to my neck, brushing my hair out of the way. He presses a soft, tender kiss to my nape that makes me swoon. My eyes float closed, and I relish the warm tingles that spread over my skin.

"I can take it slow, Sierra," he says softly as he kisses me.

I take a beat, savoring the haze of bliss surrounding

me. Then I grab the protection from the pocket, set the purse down on the nightstand, and swivel around, crawling onto the bed. I thrust the wrapper at him. "Don't you dare take it slow," I say, giving a clear command.

He threads his hand through my hair, gripping the back of my head. "You sure you know what you like?"

"I do."

Chance tugs on my hair again, pulling me closer. His possessive touch sends small pinpricks of blissful pain through my body—a pain I crave.

He loosens the grip. "Tell me then. I'm game for anything you want."

Images dance through my head. The array of videos I've watched over the years. "So many things turn me on," I admit.

His grin is wicked as he pulls me onto his lap, wrapping my legs around his waist, urging me to grind against his hard-on.

"I'm listening," he says in a low rumble as his hands curl tightly over my hips, his thumbs digging into my bones. This man already knows to manhandle me and that makes me hot. A man who listens, a man who wants to give me my fantasies.

My ex had no interest in my pleasure. He had no curiosities about my dirty dreams. We never talked about sex in detail.

So, this is a first too, and I damn well want Chance to know. "I've never said these things out loud to a man," I confess as I rub my center shamelessly against the firm length of his cock.

"Good. Tell me, Sierra. I want to hear them, want to know your wishes," he murmurs, sounding desperate as he lavishes open-mouthed kisses along my neck, nipping my flesh as he goes.

He pulls back, meets my gaze, and patiently waits.

I unravel my desires for him. "I want to ride you. Hard and fast and fearlessly."

His jaw goes slack. Breath stutters. "Check," he says.

"I want you to pull my hair like you've been doing. Smack my ass. Bite my tits," I say, lust whipping through me.

His murmurs turn into a savage groan. "Done. Consider it fucking done."

My hands clasp his shoulders tightly as I rock against him. "Want you to rip off my panties."

Moaning, he slides a hand down my stomach, between our bodies. He wedges the heel of his palm against the panel of my panties, rubbing hard. "You mean these soaked panties? The ones that are absolutely useless because you're already so fucking wet?"

Lust radiates from my core out to my limbs as I pant a *yes*. "Those panties," I murmur, then, tell him another fantasy. "And I want you to fuck me on all fours."

"Woman." Chance drags a hand over his face. "We're going to need more than a few nights to make it through this Christmas list."

Yes, we will.

And I can't wait for all the naughty gifts.

Chance reaches for my cami, yanks it off in one rough tug, tosses it carelessly to the floor. "Your tits . . . I've got to worship them, Sierra."

He lowers his face to my chest, draws a nipple into his mouth and sucks. A sharp, hot jolt of pleasure shoots through my body, racing through my veins.

Grabbing his head, I jerk him against me, relishing the closeness. He rewards me with a nip of his teeth, and I shudder.

"Yes," I whisper, craving more.

I can feel him smile, like he's so damn pleased to know how much I enjoy his rough touch. He licks and drags his teeth over my sensitive skin, then bites down harder.

"Oh God," I rasp out.

I am a live wire. I am shaking everywhere. My whole body pulses.

He raises his face and grabs my hips.

I expect him to gently shift me off him, to set me on my back. Instead, he lifts me, then simply tosses me onto my stomach.

Oh. Oh yes. I like being manhandled very much.

He gets off the bed, stands at the foot. "Watch me," he says, giving a rough command.

Raising my face, I stay in place like that, on my stomach, the center of my body aching as I stare at this gorgeous man, tall, built, rippling with muscles. His chest is covered with a fine dusting of hair that travels down in a delicious happy trail to where his hands go next—the waistband of his black boxer briefs.

A drop of liquid darkens the fabric. That thrills me, knowing he's so turned on that his dick is leaking for me.

He pushes the boxers down and his cock springs

free. Hard, long, and hungry for me. Wrapping a hand around his shaft, he strokes down, once, twice. Heat pools between my legs as I stare shamelessly at his cock.

"You like that," he says. "Me stroking myself for you."

"So much," I moan. He moves from the foot of the bed around to the side. Craning my neck, I watch as he slides his hand down my back, stopping at my panties. He pulls hard on the cotton fabric, then laughs. "Sorry, Sierra. I don't think I'm going to be able to rip these off tonight. If you have lace, I can rip that tomorrow night."

"I do," I say, as a thrill rushes through me over these plans—plans for more sex, more playing.

"Good. Then for now I'll do this," he says, then lowers his face, drags the edge of my panties between his teeth, and tugs them down over my ass.

With his mouth.

I nearly die from the sexiness of the moment. When he has the panties at the edge of my ass, he presses a kiss to one cheek, then the other, before he nips my butt.

I groan like an animal. "Ahh, that feels so good."

Grabbing the fabric, he tugs them off the rest of the way, and throws them on the floor. He pushes me farther up on the bed, spreads my legs and kneads my ass. "I'm going to fuck you like this. With you on your stomach, me driving deep into you."

Climbing on the mattress, he covers me with his body, his hard cock sliding against my ass.

I tremble, pleasure ripping through me like a current. "I want that," I say, utterly desperate for his passion, his abandon.

Chance yanks me up on all fours, kneels behind me,

and plants another kiss on my cheek as he slides a hand between my thighs. I gush, heat flooding my center. I'm outrageously wet.

"Oh, gorgeous," he moans as his fingers slide through my slickness. My back bows and I move with him, seeking more of his touch.

"Please," I groan.

"You're soaked. So fucking slippery. So hot," he says, praising me as he teases my clit. Sparks shoot through me everywhere, and I'm floating high above the earth.

My mind spins, pleasure traveling through every cell as he strokes me all while kissing my ass, nipping the flesh.

Desire swirls in me.

I feel out of control.

Wild.

Desperate.

I rock into his touch. "A little harder," I urge him on. He goes faster, rougher, then he slides a finger into me.

I gasp.

"You like that?"

"I do."

Another finger, another crook of it inside me. I clench, shaking as I claw at the sheets.

He keeps that up, rubbing my clit, stroking my pussy, nipping my flesh. Ecstasy throbs in me as my climax nears, then arrives boldly, bursting through my body in a hot blur of pleasure.

"Yes, yes, yes," I shout, shaking everywhere, falling into a heap of satisfaction on the king-size bed.

Yet I'm still hungry for more.

A few seconds later, he scoops me up, pulls me into his arms, and kisses me.

It's a slow, lush kiss that makes my head feel hazy.

My chest goes woozy.

I feel drunk on pleasure.

When he breaks the kiss, he settles onto his back on the bed, grabs his cock, and slides a thumb over the head, moving a drop of liquid arousal around the crown. His eyes are hooded, glimmering with desire.

"I want to see you fuck my cock, Sierra."

Dear God. I hit the jackpot. This good guy is a filthy fucker in bed, like I've always wanted.

"I'm ready," I say, straddling him.

He reaches for the condom, opens it, slides it down his length, then pulls me to him. But before I can line up and take a man inside me for the first time in my life, he curls a hand around my face, draws me close and kisses me again. Tender and gentle. He murmurs softly as his lips explore mine. When he lets go, he whispers, "I'll fuck you hard and good, but sometimes I want to kiss you soft and gentle. Because that's how I feel for you," he says, his tone hooking into my heart.

I've chosen wisely.

I know too that I've chosen a man who doesn't just want to fuck. He feels something for me. Perhaps the same something I feel for him.

Is it just desire? Only wild lust? Or something else?

For a flash of a second, he looks at me like *this* could be more. Like there's longing. Like there's possibility.

As I straddle him, possibilities spark all through my veins, my mind, my body.

Possibilities of nights and days.

But that's all too much to consider.

Right now, I want to feel all the dirty things.

Pleasure. Just pleasure. That's all I can handle.

Taking his thick cock in my hand, I rub him against my wetness, then draw a sharp inhale.

His hand slides down my arm. "We can stop anytime if it hurts," he says.

My heart beats harder. "I love that you say that. I love that you're concerned."

"I mean it, Sierra. I want to give you everything you want, but if something doesn't feel right to you, just tell me. You mean more to me than sex," he says, so earnest that my chest squeezes.

And I feel that possibility once again. It scares me but it also electrifies me.

I look into his eyes, nodding as I lick my lips. "I promise."

To say that feels just as good as this bliss does.

Then I lower myself onto him, my breath hitching.

The first inch is full and delicious. Like when I take vibrators into my body. Then I slide down more, bring him deeper. The sensations intensify. Some are good; some are bad. I close my eyes. For a few seconds, everything in the center of my body hurts, a painful stretch.

Chance seems to sense it. "Take it slow, gorgeous," he says.

I nod, adjusting, getting used to him. To the odd sensation of being stretched wide open.

Another breath.

Letting the air fill my body and relax me, I sink

down the rest of the way. It's still strange, still intense. But soon, the pain ebbs, melts into pleasure.

Only pleasure.

And I ache for more of him.

I set my hands on his pecs. His big palms wrap tight around my hips as his gaze stays locked on my face. "Set the pace, gorgeous. Whatever you want."

I rock my hips back and forth.

Thrusting.

Swaying.

Taking.

Feeling.

So, this is sex.

So, this is fucking.

And it feels as good as it looked all those years.

That's because of the man I'm with. A man I want to get closer to. I rock and I move, swiveling my hips as he grabs me, pulling me closer.

"You feel incredible," I whisper.

His eyes are hazy, fiery. "No, you do. You feel so fucking good," he grits out.

"We do, then," I correct.

"Yeah," he says on a moan as he squeezes my ass, kneads the flesh in just the way I've been wanting.

He hauls me in for a deep, possessive kiss. Pleasure shoots through me everywhere, coiling in the center of my body, flinging itself through my veins out to my toes, to my fingertips.

I feel good everywhere. So good I sense my climax isn't far away. But I want to make sure it happens. So I break the kiss, rise up, set a hand on his chest. "I'm going to play with myself," I tell him.

He groans, a savage, wild sound that echoes through the room. "Do it. I want to watch."

I slide my hand between my legs, teasing at my clit, savoring the tight, hot knot of sensations. I've had plenty of orgasms. I've given myself countless ones. He already gave me one tonight.

And I know my body, so I can tell the next one isn't far off. The exquisite ache between my legs intensifies and I stroke faster, knowing exactly how to get there.

But even though I *can* get there on my own, Chance is with me completely, thrusting deep inside my body as I rub my clit.

He's in every moment with me.

Wanting my pleasure.

Chasing it desperately too.

Sensation seizes me, commands my cells, tightens every muscle. I gasp, freezing as I shatter, bliss cascading everywhere inside me in a wild, intense orgasm that blots out the world.

I shout, calling his name, shaking.

When I'm about to collapse on him, he grabs my hips, flips me to my back, and shoves my knees up practically near my shoulders. He drives deep into me, like an animal. "Need to fuck you hard. Say it's okay."

"It's more than okay," I say, and he fucks me hard, making me feel incredible all over again as he groans, grits his teeth, then grunts, "Coming."

The man shudders.

He's always been beautiful to me.

But he's beautiful in a whole new way as he loses control inside me, coming hard, then collapsing onto me.

I smile, thrilled at the decadence, the deliciousness.

And how good we feel together. "You convinced me," I whisper playfully.

He takes a few seconds, then laughs. "All I ever wanted," he says, then hugs me tight. "And so's this."

17

CHANCE

In the shower a little later, I pour tropical body wash into my palm, then roam my hands across her shoulders, down her arms, along her stomach, smiling stupidly as I go.

She laughs softly. "Why are you grinning like that?"

I shrug, still hopped up on endorphins. "Great sex has that effect," I say.

She's quiet, and I hope that wasn't the wrong thing to say. "It *was* great," I add, reassuring her.

"Was it for you, though?" Her voice pitches up, hopeful.

Ah, she has no barometer for how a man reacts. "You were amazing. You are absolutely amazing, and the sex was incredible." I hope she loved it as much as I did. It was electric. "You don't believe me?"

Sierra takes the body wash then cleans up, keeping her hair out of the stream as she goes. "It's just all new to me," she says. "But I'm only human. I want it to be as good for you as it was for me. Because that was dream-come-true sex for me."

It's official. I can die now having completed my mission on earth—to please a woman that well. I rope a hand around her waist, haul her body against mine. "It was *earth-shattering*. Hell, I'm pretty sure my toes curled."

She grins, the kind of smile that shines in her eyes, and I'm glad I hit the right note at last. "You made my knees weak, Chance."

Pretty sure she did the same to me. And fair's fair—since she's been so open with me about her sex life, the least I can do is be the same way about mine. "To be honest, I haven't had sex like that . . ." I drift off, but my memory comes up empty. There's nothing to compare tonight to. "Honestly, I've *never* had sex like that, Sierra. Ever. It was intense. Insanely passionate."

Her eyes go soft. Her lips part. "It felt that way to me too, Chance," she says, vulnerability coloring her tone as well, and the sound causes my heart to thrum harder for her.

"Good. I wanted you to feel incredible. That was all I wanted," I say.

She loops her hands around my neck, her fingertips playing with my wet hair. "I've watched a lot of videos. Read a lot about sex. I had a pretty good idea of what I wanted. But being with you felt better than I even imagined."

Being with you.

Those words reverberate. "Same for me, gorgeous.

That was better than I imagined. And trust me, I've thought a lot about sleeping with you."

Her eyes sparkle with delight.

I have more to say, though, tonight is a time for total honesty, it seems. "You're only the second woman I've been with," I tell her.

Her mouth falls open. "Wow. I had no idea."

Talking about Natasha isn't my favorite thing to do. But these details feel important for Sierra to know, especially given what she's shared with me. "My ex and I met in college. We were together for a long time. We were each other's firsts. But the sex faded a lot the last few years we were together, and honestly, even before then, it was never like that." I wave in the direction of the bed —the scene of the white-hot crime of . . . fantastic sex.

As the water beats down on us, Sierra arches a dubious brow. "Never? Really?"

I hold up a hand. "Scout's honor."

She shoves me gently on my wet pecs. "You were never a Boy Scout."

"Pitcher's honor, then," I say, wiggling a brow. "Closing pitcher's honor, to be precise."

Tilting her head, a little saucily, she smiles. "Fine. I believe you now."

"Good. You should."

I take the soap and wash up, sharing even more with her. "But I've wanted that kind of abandon in bed. To be rough, be wild. Your fantasies match mine. But I never had the chance to act on them till you."

Sierra takes a breath, maybe gearing up to say something hard. "I want to sleep with you again. What do you think? Want a couple encores?"

What I think is I've won the World Series again. I think I've struck sex gold. "Hmm. Seems just like I convinced you to root for the Cougars, and you've convinced me to go for seconds and thirds," I tease.

She rolls her eyes, swats my shoulder this time. "*Chance.*"

I pull her close. "I want you again and again, Sierra."

"Sounds like a great plan for the next twenty-four or so hours," she says.

I freeze under the hot water.

Twenty-four hours?

That's it? Give or take, that's all I have with her?

Of course it is. We're both leaving the morning after the wedding. Returning to being...part of the same circle.

And yet I already know I want this fling to last beyond two nights in paradise. I'll have to figure out how the hell to maneuver that.

For now, though, I'm going to enjoy the fuck out of spending the night with her close to me.

I stop the water, and we dry off then get into bed. Under the covers, with the terrace door open and the rhythmic sounds of the ocean lapping against the shore, I run a hand along her arm. I'm unable to stop touching her. "That couch did look ridiculously uncomfortable."

She gives me a flirty, dirty look. "Confession: you were never going to sleep on that couch," she whispers. "From the moment we walked into this suite today, I had plans for you, Chance. I've wanted it to be you for a lot longer than just today."

I eat up her compliments. "How long?"

She stares at the ceiling, taps her chin. "Remember the night you walked me home?"

"Hell, yeah. I was so damn tempted to invite myself up," I say.

"I knew for sure then that I wanted you to be my first," she says, reminiscing, tripping back to a happy memory.

I'm all warm and buzzy. "But I think we needed to get *here,* in Hawaii, for it to happen."

"True, but I've had my eye on you for a while, Chance," she says, settling into the pillows, like it's a relief to admit this attraction at last.

Hell, it is to me too. For months, the desire has brewed inside me. "I would come by The Spotted Zebra with the guys, but I always wanted to see you."

"We could chat about the day or baseball or books or comedies."

She grins, propping her head into her hand as she shifts to her side. "Everything was so easy with us. Still is."

Easy. This is just nice and easy here in bed, and then we'll return to nice and easy in San Francisco too.

But still, I'm not sure twenty-four hours will satiate me. For now though, I'll take what I can get.

18

CHANCE

The next morning, I rouse as the sun filters in, its rays luring me from slumber. The other side of the bed is empty. My gaze sails around the suite.

Sierra stands at the terrace, drinking in the view of the ocean, looking peaceful.

I swing my legs out of bed, pull on a pair of shorts, and join her on the deck. She wears a bikini top and a sarong, looking like a vacation goddess. It's a good view. No idea where we go from here, or what happens next. But for now, I move behind her, brush her hair from her neck, kiss her there. She sighs happily and rests her head against my shoulder. "Good morning, handsome," she says.

"Now it is," I say, as I loop my arms around her waist and stare at the ocean spreading all the way to the horizon. "What a view."

"I like *that* view too." She points to the beach below us and a little lagoon at the edge of the resort. A woman in a red one-piece suit drags surfboards into the small cove, setting them on the water so they float peacefully. "It's surfboard yoga and it's calling my name."

"Huh. What do you know? Mine too. My contract forbids me from going surfing. But I could do surfboard yoga." I squeeze her butt. "I like your sense of adventure."

"I'm quite adventurous, Chance," she says, with a twinkle in her eyes.

"I noticed that last night."

And I want to experience her again.

As I put on board shorts, I work through options that might earn us an extension on our arrangement past Hawaii. Maybe I need to talk to TJ, or to Google, and ask how to keep a fling going beyond the initial time frame and still return to friendship when it's over.

For now, though, it's time to yoga the fuck out of a surfboard.

* * *

I do my damnedest to stretch like a cat, a cow, a downward-facing dog. But on an upward dog, I stumble, splashing into the water. Sierra cracks up and offers me a hand, but I shake it off. I pop back up on the board, all wet, and thoroughly determined to nail this pose.

I get on my hands and feet, arching my spine. The view is distracting, though, because Sierra looks phenomenal in her purple bikini, showing off her moves on that surfboard.

I get in the zone, though, and apply my laser focus to the pose. But I find a way to multitask, sneaking peeks at the woman by my side who is sharing a perfect day with me.

I want another day like this. Hell, make it a few more.

How to get them is the question.

* * *

When we finish the class, we go for a hike on a nearby trail, walking through the lush resort gardens. Sierra's wearing the pink cap I bought her, and if a hat can make me feel possessive of a woman, this one is doing the trick.

Decked out in a gift I got her, she feels a bit like mine, and I don't mind this feeling.

As we meander through the foliage, she tells me about the flowers we see, rattling off details on the hibiscus and birds of paradise. "I have a big thing for flowers," she says with a little shrug.

"You always have a fresh bouquet at the bar. Right there at the corner, every night."

She wings a smile my way. "You're observant."

"It happens when you have a thing for the bar owner," I say. And wow, it's like a weight has been lifted. I'm free to say these things to her that have been on my mind for months.

"Right back atcha, handsome," she says. Her compliment comes out nice and easy, like maybe she's exercising the same freedom.

Maybe it's a damn good sign she'd be open to a sex fling addendum—the addition of extra days and then we return to how we were. *Friends* and *teammate's sister.*

I make a rolling gesture, signaling for her to keep talking as we walk along the path lined with ferns and hibiscus flowers. "So, tell me more about your love of all things floral."

"Well, if I was going to go all amateur psychologist on myself, I'd say it's probably because I work all the time, so I snag my little indulgences where I can—lotions and potions that smell yummy, pretty flowers, sexy lingerie."

"Mmm. I believe lace is on the menu tonight," I say.

"And you'll get it. But it's also because I just love pretty things," she says with an unapologetic grin. "And pretty-smelling things." Stopping, she points to a white flower. "Like those gardenias. Want to test your nose? Tell me what you smell."

The competitor in me takes the stage as I bend to inhale the scent. "Kind of velvety and fragrant."

"Velvety is right. Let's see. How else can I put your nose to the test?"

I rope an arm around her waist, yanking her back to my chest so I can run my nose through her soft hair. "How's this? You smell like blackberry, a hint of pineapple, and all my dirty thoughts."

"You're passing with flying colors."

I spin her around and steal a kiss in the middle of the flowers.

"Mmm," she says, returning the favor. "And you have that soapy, woodsy, I-want-you-to-bend-me-over-the-bed smell."

I laugh. "And we officially have aced the nose test."

She turns, and we continue on the path. I gesture to some plants along the way. "Want me to wow you with my plant knowledge? *Boom*—plumeria."

She slow claps. "Your new nickname is Chance 'Green Thumb' Ashford."

I raise a finger to make a point. "I'll have you know I take excellent care of an entire bullpen of succulents at my place."

A brow lifts in question. "A bullpen?"

Am I doing this? Telling her about one of my quirks?

And the answer is yes. This conversation is more fun than I've had in ages. "Yes, they're named Mariano, Trevor Hoffman and Dennis Eckersley. The three greatest closers of all time."

"But only Mariano goes by just his first name?"

I scoff, like *isn't it obvious*. "Of course. He's one-name-only worthy. The best of all time. But I named them all since I believe in paying homage to the greats who make my life possible."

"And you do that by naming plants after them? That's insanely adorable."

"Please don't tell opposing batters I'm adorable," I say with a growl.

She stops to pat my cheek. "I will keep all your secrets, you chocolate-covered-strawberry-loving, plant-naming, pink-hat-buying, fearsome closing pitcher who strikes fear into his opponents when he stalks to the mound in the ninth inning."

I narrow my eyes, adopt the sternest expression in

the history of stony looks. "Just like that," I say, in a low rumble.

"If they only knew you were a softie underneath," she teases.

I grab her arm and yank her against me, her lush body pressed to mine. "You will tell no one that I name plants." I drop my voice to a bare whisper. "Or that I talk to them."

"Shut up. You talk to your plants?"

"I ask them to watch over me as I pitch," I whisper.

"The fact that you talk to your plants is my new favorite thing about you." She coasts her hands up my chest, cupping my face. "You. Are. Criminally. Cute."

I crack up, and we kiss again, laughing as we do.

That's a great way to kiss, I'm discovering. Kissing and laughing, feeling like you connect with someone. It warms my jaded, bruised heart. Makes me feel like we can have this fling, and go right back to friendship and guy codes and all the good things.

But first, I'd like a few more nights please. No reason for a sex fling to only last two short nights, after all.

Maybe that's how I'll make my pitch to tack on some extra days. A *why not?* proposition.

Striking out the side with the bases loaded is easier than figuring out how to broach my desire for more of her. I have zero experience in navigating unconventional arrangements with a woman.

But sex? That's throwing a fastball down the middle, so I laser in on that when we return to the suite. I bend her over the bed, take her again, and give her an epic orgasm, enjoying one helluva climax myself.

Afterward, we fall onto the mattress in a tangle of limbs, sweat, and breath.

I love Hawaii.

* * *

When Sierra and I head down to the beach for Trish and Blake's sunset ceremony, we hold hands, like we did last night.

When I get my first chance during the reception, I snag a minute away from her. I grab my brother, catching TJ up on the details.

"So you want to have a longer sex fling?" he asks.

It sounds so crass when he puts it like that. *Sex fling*. But I'm not entirely sure how to put into words what I want, so I try to keep it simple. "I'd like to spend more time with her. Yes."

A soft chuckle is his answer. "Sex. More time," he says, like tomato, toe-mah-toe. "Whatever helps you sleep at night, baby bro. Point being, you want a longer . . . *fling*." TJ sketches air quotes.

I want an extension. For sex, yes, but also for going on hikes and talking about plants and flowers. Which sounds like . . . exactly what I can't say to anyone, even my brother.

"Yes, a longer fling," I reply.

With a thoughtful sigh, he scrubs his jaw. "None of this one-night-only stuff. Right?"

"Exactly."

Like he's the relationship guru, TJ parks a hand on my shoulder. "Here's what I'd do if I were writing this scene in a book. I'd have the hero figure out what's in it for her. How to make it work in her life. Because the last thing you want is to come across like a horny, sex-starved, walking boner who just wants to get laid."

Whoa. "Tell me what you really think."

He smirks. "Then don't come across that way to her."

I'm still not in the market for anything permanent, but last night with Sierra felt like sex, passion, and intimacy.

It felt like a real connection. Like we understood each other's needs.

And right then, I know how to ask for what I want.

19

SIERRA

Staring is not acceptable at most social gatherings, but it's required at weddings.

I gawk happily at the bride as Trish sways with Blake on the dance floor under the tent by the edge of the Pacific.

In her flowy wedding dress, with hibiscuses in her hair, the bride laughs, then presses a kiss to Blake's lips.

My heart patters. Hell, maybe it pitters too. From my spot at the bar, I sigh happily, drinking a glass of wine while Chance chats with his parents and his brother on the lawn. I can't imagine my parents behaving well with each other at someone else's wedding.

But then, my parents are the epitome of behaving badly. Always fighting. Shouting insults.

They didn't get along with each other when Grant and I were growing up. I doubt they could be in the same venue now without hissing at each other like two alley cats. Meanwhile, the past and present Ashfords are laughing and toasting. They're all good guys and good women.

Maybe that's why Chance is so focused on his code. That's all he knows, all he's seen. He could teach a class in how to get along with everyone.

But then, he sure as hell tossed out that code in sinful style last night.

And I am damn glad we exercised the bro code loophole.

Slivers of the two of us coming together flash before my eyes—skin, bodies, moans. Names whispered at the edge of passion.

I draw a sharp breath, heating up.

"Busted!" a bright voice chirps in my ear.

Startled, I turn to the platinum-haired maid of honor, all big green eyes and a yellow dress. I flap my hand at Clementine's attire. "You're the only person in the universe who can wear yellow and look good."

"It's almost a fashion injustice," another voice chimes in, smooth and alto. That's Skyler, another one of our crew from San Francisco who flew down for the wedding. I haven't seen her in a while, so I pull her close for a hug.

"Good to see you," I say to the personal stylist. Skyler shops for people who hate shopping. Translation—she has a long client list.

"You too. And you look fabulous, as well, in your sexy pink dress," she says, taking in the dusty-rose sundress that swirls just below my knees.

Clementine steps closer. "And I think I know why

our Sierra looks so good," she says in a cat-ate-the-canary tone.

I grin, since it's useless to hide my smile, though I play it coy as I ask, "And why's that, Clem?"

My dog-loving friend nudges my elbow. "Is someone getting some?"

A wiggle of Skyler's brows comes next. "Tell us everything."

I grab their arms, pull them away from the bar and toward a hammock at the edge of the grounds. "Yes, is it obvious?"

Skyler studies my face and nods sagely. "You have a very just-been-fucked look about you," she deadpans.

A dirty thrill rushes through me, and I touch my cheek. "And what is that exactly?"

Clementine grins like a naughty kid. "You're all glowy. Dewy. Shiny."

I crack up. "You sound like a face cream commercial."

"Sex is good for the skin," Skyler deadpans.

"Then I better have an amazing complexion," I whisper.

"Get it, girl," Clementine says, then makes a rolling gesture with her hands. "Spill the tea. How was it?"

A zip of pleasure rushes through me from the memory of last night and this afternoon. I'm bursting to tell my girlfriends. "It was amazing. I never knew sex could be so incredible. It's basically better than . . . well, music, food, drinks, and even cats."

Clementine throws her arms around me and we all squeal.

"Sex is the best," Skyler says when Clementine and I separate. "Fine, it's been a year for me, but if memory serves, it was something I rather enjoyed . . ."

"It's something I *want* to enjoy," Clementine puts in.

I meet her gaze and deliver the best advice a recently deflowered gal can give. "And you should enjoy it to the fullest. And find a man who wants to give you what you ask for. I basically told Chance what I wanted, and he delivered. Sex is awesome with a man you like. A man who listens. A man who wants to please you."

Clementine dances a jig. "A man who listens? He's a keeper for sure."

I tense at that word. *Keeper* cuts the moment in half, slicing away the lightness, hitting pause on my happy-go-horny mood. "He's not a keeper. I didn't mean it like that. He's not interested in anything long-term," I say, my voice a little wobblier than I'd like.

But why is it hard to speak the truth? I shouldn't be bothered to voice the backbone of our arrangement. Neither one of us wants more than a quick fling. That's what we agreed to.

Except I'm starting to wonder what *more* would look like.

Skyler sighs, gives a sympathetic look. "Bummer."

I shake my head, dismissing her worries. "Oh, it's totally fine. I don't want anything long-term either," I say, though I wouldn't mind more days with Chance, more time with him. Last night was everything I imagined. But today? The time with him wandering along the hiking trail, checking out flowers and plants, was even better. I never knew it was possible to make love like that, and then to laugh, tease, and play so easily.

My heart warms as my gaze wanders to Chance once again, standing at the edge of the tent. He tosses his head back, laughing at something his mom says. A smile takes over my whole being, unbidden. He's just so good with people. He's good with me. He's the sexiest, funniest, sweetest guy I know.

I tear my gaze away and turn back to my friends so I don't get lost in this new haze of longing. "Anyway, it's all good. Chance and I have an arrangement, and we agreed on it," I say, as chipper as I can be and focused on the facts. Just the facts.

Not these flutters of feelings.

"Good thing you agree," Skyler says, going along with it. "Yay you then!"

But Clementine seems suspicious, tilting her head as she peers at me. "You're truly fine with it, Sierra? I always thought you had a big crush on him. And that's risky in these situationships."

"Well, I did have a crush," I say, then backpedal, trying to make sense of this new bloom of emotions. "I mean, I do. Wait. Is it still a crush if you're sleeping with him in said situationship?"

We're all quiet, the three of us looking back and forth at each other, then drifting off to the ocean for answers.

Is this still a crush?

Has it already turned into something else? My rushing pulse and squishy heart suggest it has.

But what?

I don't know what *this* is, or what it should be. I have no answers to the question of what to do with my runaway feelings.

Clementine clears her throat, more solemn than usual as she says, "You'll know it was a crush if it doesn't truly hurt when it ends."

Skyler nods immediately, her tone a little heavy too. "Truer words."

Great. Just great. Now I'm thinking of endings and hurting rather than good times and pleasure. The goddamn point of this no-strings fling is that we won't hurt each other. "Then it's simply a crush," I say, chin up, brave face on, trying to remember the rules of engagement. "Let's go back."

I gesture to the tent, and we return to the party. When I reach the dance floor, a hand touches my arm, feeling familiar, but not quite.

I spin around—the face of the man is familiar too. The face of the man I slept with. But I meet his eyes and, though almost identical, I spot the difference.

But it's not Chance. It's TJ.

"Hey, Sierra," he says with only a sliver of a smile. "Want to dance?"

"Sure," I say, but the truth is . . . I'm unsure. He looks more intense than I'd expect.

We head out to the dance floor, shaking it to a fast song, making small talk about one of his books. "My favorite scene in *Come Again* is the one in the bakery—when he takes her to Piece of Cake, and she's moaning and groaning around the mouthful like it's foreplay."

"She wasn't wrong," he deadpans.

"Nor were you. I love that you can get inside the mind of both a man and a woman."

"Thank you," he says, clearly sincere. "That means a lot to me. Truly it does."

I screw up the corner of my lips. "Funny—you and Chance sound a lot alike, but I can tell your voices apart by the way you speak, how the sentences come together. Yours are almost more . . . observational. Which sort of makes sense, since that's what you do."

He smiles for a second. "That does make sense." But then his humor vanishes as the song winds down. TJ locks his eyes with mine like I'm in his crosshairs. "So listen, Sierra . . ."

Nerves prickle through me from the intensity that's purely TJ. "Yes?"

"You seem great. I like you. So does Chance."

"I like him too," I say. Where is he going with this?

"Good." He takes a beat. "Don't break his heart, then." It's an order, crisp and clear from the minutes-older brother. Then TJ brushes a kiss onto my cheek. "Good dancing with you and chatting books. I look forward to grabbing a drink at your bar when I'm in the city."

He walks away.

What was the deal with that warning? Is he simply being a big brother? Or is there something more at play? I don't have much time to contemplate, because his twin heads my way, smiling like he has a secret. This is whiplash, even though I'm wildly happy to see Chance. My bones hum as he nears me. My chest flips. I am so into him, it's crazy.

This feeling is wild and wonderful, and I want to embrace it.

Chance reaches me as the music shifts to a slow song. "May I have this dance?"

"You may," I say, feeling fluttery and warm.

I let TJ's warning fade away as Chance wraps his hands around my waist. We dance to the love song under the Hawaiian sky. His eyes twinkle, and he sure looks like he has an ace up his sleeve.

I'm about to ask what's up when Chance spins me around, dips me, then says, "I have a proposition for you."

Color me intrigued. "Hit me up," I say, my hair spilling toward the floor.

He yanks me up, running a hand along the cherry tattoo on my arm. "You said you were going to Las Vegas when you return."

"Yes, I did," I say, curious as to why he's asking.

"At the risk of inviting myself along, I'd love to invite myself along. I could spend more time with you as you check out your bartender and comic. Get us a luxury suite at The Extravagant if you'd like. Treat you to another few days of the vacation you deserve. Go to clubs if you want. Soak in the jacuzzi. Order room service and then lavish you in orgasms all night long." He takes a beat, twirls me, then drags me in close, his big body pressed to mine.

My skin tingles. My heart trips along.

That invitation sounds like we're zooming well past the crush zone. We're racing into more than a fling.

Every single thing he's suggesting tantalizes me. I do

need a vacation. A few more days treating myself—or really, being treated—would be good for me.

But that's not why I want to take him up on his offer.

I want as much of Chance as I can get. I want to gobble up all the time he's offering. To indulge in as much of my crush as possible.

Even if it'll hurt when it ends.

"I'd say that's the best self-invitation I've ever heard. I will RSVP right now."

A rumble coasts across his lips as I grab the collar of his shirt and bring him close for a tropical kiss. A kiss that makes me want to drag him away from the wedding right now. But we can't escape till later.

So after the cake and more toasts and more dancing, I seize the opportunity I desperately want to be alone with him. "Want to get out of here?"

Chance's eyes flicker. "More than I've ever wanted any chocolate-covered strawberry in my life."

High praise, indeed.

20

CHANCE

My mission is singular—make myself scarce ASAP.

As we walk around the tent, I acquire the target—a path winding between the palm trees that leads to the hotel entrance, aka, our escape hatch.

Which leads to our suite.

That's where I want to be.

With Sierra's hand in mine, I walk quickly.

Avoiding my parents.

Avoiding Natasha.

Avoiding everyone.

But when I reach the edge of the spongy grass, footsteps crunch in the night. I snap my gaze to my left. Jordy ambles over, bright gratitude in his blue eyes. Stopping at my side, he spreads his arms out wide. "You save baseball games, and you saved my sorry ass last night. Rockstar closer," he booms. "Bring it in."

Damn. I want to be in the fucking room. Instead, I give my cousin a hug and he hugs me back harder. "What would I have done without you?"

"Spent the night puking in the plumeria?" I suggest.

"Exactly. I owe you big time, bud."

We break apart, and I slug his shoulder. "You're all good, man," I say, and flash him a grin.

Sierra does the same. "Glad you're feeling better, Jordy."

His bushy eyebrows shoot into his hairline. "Oh, my bad! You're with your lady. Sorry, big-ass sorry!" He eyes Sierra up and down and hums approvingly. "Way to upgrade, Chance. Very, very nice."

I bristle. "Don't talk that way about women. They aren't cars."

Jordy shrugs with a smile. "It was a compliment. I like cars and I like babes." He turns to Sierra. "You're prettier than his ex. And you're also nicer. She never once asked if I was feeling better after a glass of wine."

"Well, thank you for the compliment. I enjoy cars as well. And I'm glad you're having a good time," she says, handling Jordy like the bartender pro she is—smooth and good-natured, a kind word for everyone.

But Sierra *truly* is this person. She legitimately cares. She's the opposite of Natasha, who was all farce, all online persona.

Sierra is the same woman behind the bar and away from it—fiery and clever, loving and fierce, kind and strong. A person who gives a shit about people.

She's the real deal.

My heart kicks a little faster.

I will it to settle down. Now isn't the time for flutters. Or for adding up all her pros. "We're having a great time," I put in.

"Best wedding ever," Jordy adds, not to be outdone. He claps me on the shoulder, his expression turning a touch concerned. "And you're doing well, my man. You're obviously over . . . *the Bitchy McWitch*." He dips his voice. "But how was it seeing Trish walk down the aisle with Natasha right there? And with that Doofus McDickhead she's with now watching from his seat?" He mimes gagging. "I have to see my ex at work all the time and it's brutal. Carve my heart up with a chainsaw. But you—you doing okay?"

I traveled to Hawaii expecting this question.

I prepped for it.

Hell, *that* question is the very reason Sierra's here. As a shield for people like Jordy who have no filter.

But the answer is remarkably easy, just like it was when Blake asked last night. Like it was when Natasha poked her head out at the party too. Turns out seeing the woman I devoted a decade of my life to feels a lot like . . . nothing.

Just nothing.

And that's wonderful.

"You know, I feel great," I tell Jordy from the heart.

A heart that's filling up again, making space for someone else.

I loop an arm around Sierra's waist, tugging her close. This contact isn't make-believe, though. I don't do it to show off a fake date.

I'm touching her because I want to.

Because she makes a day great and a night even better.

Turned out I didn't need protection from uncomfortable questions. I've been over my ex for a long time. Since well before we divorced.

Maybe what I truly needed was an excuse to finally ask Sierra out.

After we say goodbye to Jordy, Sierra and I head into the hotel. Like I've drunk too much caffeine, I'm jazzed to tell her what I just realized. "Funny thing," I say, my words spilling out. "I thought I would need you here as a buffer. I thought it would really bug me if people asked me about her."

"Does it?"

I shake my head. "Not one single bit."

"Because I'm here?"

"Yes, and because . . ." I shrug, big and wide. "I don't care if anyone asks about her. I've been over her for a long time. They can say whatever they want. It's like when someone says *sucks that you lost the playoffs*."

A slow smile spreads across her face. "It's just life."

"Just one of those things, and it's fine."

"So you didn't *need* me after all," she says, bright and cheery, like she's proud of me.

But my *personal growth* isn't the point I want to make with Sierra.

I stop in the hall, meet her gaze, run a hand down her cherry tree ink. This isn't what I planned. I don't know how this thing with us will play out in a few more days. But for now, I need to say *this*. "No, I didn't need you as a fake date. But it turns out I *want* you . . . as a real date."

In her gaze, I see new possibilities. I see so much

more than I expected when we got on that plane yesterday. And I've no idea where our flight is headed.

"That's all I want too," she says softly.

It feels like we're traveling to a new destination. But it's entirely a mystery where we're going.

21

CHANCE

When we reach the suite, I open the door at the speed of sound, then kick it closed.

I shove her up against the wall and devour her mouth. Sierra laid out her desires from the start. She wants it a little rough, a bit commanding. She wants her man to take her as soon as we walk into the hotel room.

That's what she'll get from me.

As I claim her lips, she utters a plaintive, needy sound that drives me on. My tongue explores her mouth with possession, with the kind of intensity the two of us want to have together. I suck her bottom lip between mine, giving her a hot kiss that sends fire through my veins.

She rocks against me, her hips seeking me out. That's my cue to break the kiss so I can hike up her dress, yank it over her head.

"Gorgeous," I say reverently as I step back to admire the sight in front of me—Sierra Blackwood in matching bra and panties, a dusty rose shade of lace. A groan works its way up my chest as I flick my fingers against the fabric of her panties. "I do believe I promised I would rip these off."

"And you better make good on it," she says.

I drop down to my knees, tug at the fabric, jerking it away from her body. I rip it right along the seams, and it tears with a satisfying sound.

She gasps.

Dirty delight fills my mind as I pull the remains of her panties down to the floor, then bury my face between her thighs.

She grabs my head, rocks her hips against my mouth.

My whole body vibrates as I lick and suck, flicking my tongue along the delicious rise of her clit. Digging my thumbs into her hip bones, I eat her like a starving man. She is all I need for sustenance. Her taste floods my tongue as she thrusts against me, curling her fingers tighter around my head as she murmurs words of bliss.

Yes.

Oh God.

That. Do that.

Her moans tell me to keep going. To keep giving her everything she wants. My body vibrates with the desire to please her, to send her over the edge.

I lick and suck and French kiss her pussy until her legs are shaking, until her cries of pleasure echo across the property.

She jerks me harder and fucks my face till she calls out, "*Coming.*"

Bliss runs rampant as I taste her pleasure on my tongue.

It drives me wild, and I can't stop moaning as I lap her up.

But soon, I let go, grip her hips to steady her, then rise. I plant a soft, tender kiss on her neck and travel to her ear. "You taste incredible," I whisper.

She breathes out heavily, her eyes glossy, her face flushed. "I want to know how you taste."

"That can be arranged," I say, and I'm giddy, fucking giddy, about the pending blow job. I don't think I've ever been more excited for one.

I can't wait to experience her mouth.

Because it's Sierra.

A minute later, my clothes are on the floor. Don't know where, don't care. Sinking onto the edge of the bed, I spread my legs as she gets down on her knees.

Such a beautiful position for this woman and me.

"Confession: I've been thinking about sucking your cock for a long time," she says, so deliciously dirty as she stares at my face then my aching cock.

I whimper. Is this my life? Can this decadence never end? "Let's find out if doing is better than thinking," I say, toying with the lush strands of her hair.

"Let's." She dips her face to my dick, and the second she wraps a hand around the base and licks the head, I have the answer—doing is infinitely better than imagining.

Especially when Sierra draws me into her mouth, licking as she takes me in.

My whimpers turn to moans, then wild grunts as I shake with pleasure. "That's so fucking good," I rasp out.

It's not going to take me long at all. I'm so amped up from going down on her. So aroused from being near her all night long.

I'm already close as she gazes up at me. Fire sparks in those light brown eyes as she grins wickedly.

With a hand around her head, I gently urge her to take me a little deeper. Her naughty smile grows wider as she swallows me farther.

I shudder at the sight. "That's right, gorgeous. You look so good like that," I tell the beauty at my feet.

The woman seems to want to show off, licking and sucking with fervor as she runs her palms up and down my thighs, watching my face the whole time.

She doesn't look away, and her filthy gaze turns me on more.

With a firm hand cupped around the back of her head, I thrust a little harder, pump a little deeper. The pleasure intensifies, coiling tightly in my stomach, then just bursts through my body. I don't even have time to warn her as my climax barrels down my spine.

But she doesn't seem to need one. She swallows my release with a throaty purr, and I groan for days. Starbursts spark behind my eyes as I pant and gasp, bathing in the truly fantastic orgasm.

Sierra lets go of me with a loud pop, climbs up, then wraps her arms around me. I toss her on her back. "Can I kiss you?"

"Of course." She laughs.

We taste like the kind of deep, wild connection I've never had. I don't know what we are, or what we're doing. All I know is I don't want us to end.

Closing a game is so much easier than figuring out how to have the woman I want, and follow my code too.

22

SIERRA

There's one hour till I leave for the city of sin, so as I prep food and cat litter in my apartment, I give my main man some love.

"Lynn will pop by tonight, so behave. Be a gentleman for the cat sitter," I tell Tom as I set his favorite kibble on the counter.

He purrs louder, rubbing his side against my legs.

"I know it's hard for you to be good with the ladies, but do your best. Maybe she'll introduce you to her new foster cat. I met her—and Lady Cat is gorgeous."

His rumbles intensify.

"But she'll probably find a home soon," I tell him. Lynn lives down the hall and fosters for a local rescue. Her newest is a gorgeous Siamese kitty. "I bet you wouldn't be able to keep your paws off her if you saw her," I coo.

He presses his side against my calf, which is cat for, *You're soooo right*.

I bend to scratch his chin. "Of course I'll miss you.

But I'll be back soon and"—I drop my voice to a conspiratorial whisper—"I got you a new catnip mouse."

Tom cranks up the purr-o-meter. I kiss his head, sighing happily. "You're a good boy. And thank you for understanding I need a little downtime."

He lifts his front paws, setting them on my legs, asking for me to pick him up. I give in, naturally, nuzzling him for a few minutes. "Okay, love. Soon it'll be you and me. For now, I'm going to pack."

Zoey is in charge of the bar while I'm gone, like we planned when I scheduled the trip. Last night at The Spotted Zebra, she grabbed me by the shoulders, pushed me out the door, and said, "Don't come back until after Vegas. And I mean that lovingly."

As I grab my suitcase, now empty of bikinis and sundresses, my phone trills. Chance's name flashes on the screen. A spark of heat zips through me.

"Hey there."

"Hey. Want to pack together?"

"On the phone?" I ask.

"Yes. On the phone."

My heart thunders. He is too sweet. "Let's do it," I say, delighted over this invitation to do such a pedestrian thing together.

As I move through my apartment, setting teddies and bras, little dresses, and sexy boots into my luggage, I cradle the phone against my ear, talking to him. "I'm almost done," I say, a little sassy.

"Beat ya! I tossed in another Henley. I'm done. Packed."

"Show-off," I say with a huff. "Also, I didn't know it

was a packing race, and I'm still loading up my bag with little lacy numbers."

"Keep going. Add more," he says intensely, like a coach encouraging me.

I yank open a drawer and grab a red bra. I snap a pic and send it to him. "Check your texts, handsome."

A few seconds later, a groan comes my way. "Pack. That. Now."

"I. Will." I drop the lace into my carry-on. "Have you talked to your bullpen? Sung lullabies to the jades and the aloes before you take off for a couple of days?"

Maybe prepping like this is risky, since it makes me feel so *couple-y* with him. That's dangerous. But he sure seems like he can't stay away from me, and I can't stay away from him. We texted all day long yesterday and saw each other last night. He came over when I closed up The Spotted Zebra, bringing Chinese food and condoms. Once inside my place, he bent me over the kitchen table and fucked the long day straight out of my mind. Then we curled up on the couch and ate cold noodles and moo shu pancakes while scrolling through Webflix as Tom stretched across Chance's legs, purring.

We never watched a show though. Sleep won over, and in the morning, Chance took off early to work out with Crosby and Harlan.

Now, here we are again.

Talking, like we do this on the reg.

I add another pair of heels as he answers me about the plants. "I reassured them all that I won't be gone any longer than I normally am during the season," he says. "They're very hardy. They don't need that much from me," he says. "But I did remind them I'm going to New York straight from Vegas so they aren't surprised when I don't return right away."

The morning I leave Vegas to return home, he jets off to New York for an event with a watchmaker. We'll spend two nights together then say goodbye.

But what happens *after* Vegas?

No idea.

I focus on the here and now. "You sound like me talking to my cat, giving him all the details of my life. Who needs more reassurance though? Dennis, Trevor or Mariano?"

He laughs. "Actually, Sandy does."

As I zip up my bag, I cycle through famous closing pitchers. I don't want to be baseball illiterate, but I come up short. "Fine. I'll just admit it. I can't think of any closers named Sandy."

"Aha. That's because Sandy isn't a closer."

Wait. Does he mean the greatest pitcher ever? "Sandy Koufax? The one and only? You named a plant after a starter? You tricked me."

"I hope you'll forgive me and that you'll understand I had to ease you into my plant collection slowly." He takes a deep breath, making an audible show of girding himself to say something hard. "But now you should know, I also have an entire starting pitcher lineup," he confesses.

I laugh, my hand flying to my mouth. "That's seriously even cuter."

"So I'm cute *and* I'm adorable. Hmm."

"The cutest and the most adorable."

He sighs happily. "Some men might be bothered by those adjectives, but I asked Google if it's a compliment that a beautiful, brilliant babe calls you cute and it said yes."

"Did you really ask Google?"

"I did."

Okay, that's even more adorable. He's almost too delicious. "Tell me more about your starting lineup right now. I need to know everything. Who is in it?"

As I wheel my suitcase to the door, he rattles off the details. "I've got a hens-and-chicks named Don Drysdale. I have a burro's tail named Nolan Ryan. And the aloe vera is Pedro Martinez."

"And do you talk to them as well? Ask them to watch over you on the mound?" I ask, hoping he says yes. That'd be another thing we have in common—I talk to my cat, he talks to his plants.

"Actually, I ask them to help me be a good teammate. Something I strive to do every day." His tone is serious, a marked shift from seconds ago.

That's so sweet that I murmur an *aww*. "That's lovely, Chance. And I suspect you're a great teammate," I say, my heart beating a little faster as he opens up to me about his career.

I flash back to the comments he made about Natasha on the plane. How she didn't support his job. But I do, and I want him to know that. "I bet all the guys see you that way too. They rely on you. You bring so much to the team."

He's quiet for a few seconds. "I hope so. I hope

what's happening between you and me doesn't change things."

What's happening.

I want to clutch those words, hold them close to my heart. They seem to mean so much more than a fling. They seem to suggest something special is *what's happening.*

But those aren't the words I key in on first.

A knot of tension winds tighter in me. "Change things with my brother? Is that what you mean? Change things with all the Cougars?"

"Yes," he says heavily. "I don't want to be the guy who rocks the boat, you know? Who messes with the team chemistry?"

"We're not doing anything wrong. We're still on the same page, Chance. And really, what changed? Grant already knows we went to the wedding together on a fake date," I say, but I don't feel convinced from my words.

This isn't fake dating with Chance.

This is real dating. And we both know it.

"But it's not fake anymore, Sierra," he says, calling me on that. "That's why I worry."

If he's looking to me for reassurance that this fling is okay, I don't know that I can give it to him. I do my best, though. "But we both know the score, right? Just a few more nights together," I say, but can't bring myself to add *since neither one of us wants more.*

Since, well, I want more.

Another pause. Another heavy breath. "Of course we

do," he says, like he's injecting cheer into his voice. "And we're going to have a great time in Vegas."

"We're going to have the best time. And speaking of, I'll swing by in the Lyft and pick you up on the way," I say.

"Can't wait to see you."

After I hang up, I return to his comments about the team and how he wants to do right by the guys. Wants to follow his code. Should I let my brother know that his teammate and I are taking a trip? I certainly don't need to disclose we slept together. That's private and none of Grant's business. But am I keeping a secret if I don't tell my brother we're heading out of town for a few days?

I hover my thumb over my text thread with Grant. He's still in Hawaii on his first vacation with Declan. I don't want to bother him with my stuff.

And really, does Grant need to know about Vegas?

No. I'm a grown woman. I'm allowed to take a trip with his teammate.

Besides, Chance and I have an expiration date. Surely, this situationship will end of its own accord when we return from Vegas.

Ugh.

The thought is a punch in the gut, and I need a friend to soothe the pain. I switch over to my texts with Clementine.

Sierra: Hey . . . I need to talk to you.

Clementine: Uh-oh. What's up?

I close my eyes, set a hand on my heart, try to calm it down. Then I open my eyes and type.

Sierra: I think I really like Chance.

Two seconds later, my phone rings. In the background, a warbly voice announces the next flight is leaving Maui in twenty minutes. She must be on her way home from the wedding.

"Hey," I say. "Sorry to bug you while you're at the airport."

"Nonsense. I always have time for you. So you really like him," she repeats.

"I do, and we're about to go to Vegas," I say, swallowing past the knot in my throat.

"And it makes you sad? You sound really sad, sweetie."

"I feel that way right now," I say, but I also feel foolish. I shouldn't have any fluttery feelings about a sex getaway. That's all this is. Yet it hardly seems like one now.

"You can still have fun with him. Just focus on that. But are you sure he doesn't want anything more?"

"That's what he said. That's what I said too. So, I've got to take him at his word."

She sighs heavily. "Just guard your heart then. But you've always been good at that. It's second nature for you."

"Is it?" I ask, surprised by her swift assessment.

She scoffs. "Sierra, you've been like that ever since I've known you. You learned early how to keep your guard up. And you use it wisely. I never worry about you getting hurt. You're so tough."

I've had to be tough because of my parents. Because of the way I grew up. They're the reason I'm not impulsive. They're the reason I work my ass off. They're the reason I'm always looking out for myself.

Going away with Chance is impulsive, though, and I like this impulsive part of me.

I like this part of me that cares about another person. I like the part of me that's starting to have feelings for him.

Because I do want a little more.

I want more than sex.

I want *him*.

My throat tightens with emotion. This was supposed to be a crush, but after only a few short days in Hawaii, I'm already longing for something deeper.

Trouble is, I'm not sure he'll let himself move beyond a fling with me.

So, I'll go to Vegas and do my best to live in the here and now. If Chance and I won't last beyond this tryst, I'll make sure to savor every last second with him.

I wipe away my emotions.

I am in the Vegas zone.

23

CHANCE

As I lock the door to my home and head out, the sweet soprano voice of a six-year-old floats up from the street. "Silver! We can do silver this time, Daddy."

"*We? We,* sweetheart? There was no we about that. That was a sleep sneak attack by *you,*" Harlan says to his daughter.

"And you loved it. You left the color on all week."

"Because it looked darn fine," he says proudly.

As I bound down the steps, I lift a hand to say hi to my friend and his kid. They live a block away, so I run into them often. "How about gold, Abby? Do you think your dad's toes would look good in gold?"

Her bright eyes light up. "Gold. And silver, and bronze, and rose gold," she adds, counting off.

Harlan just shrugs easily, gesturing to the end of the street. "We're going shopping for nail polish now."

Abby squares her tiny shoulders. "So I can give Daddy a manicure too," she declares.

I bend to get eye-level with the curly-haired

brunette. "Be sure to buy scissors. Cut his hair next," I whisper.

She claps. "Ooh, that's such a good idea. Daddy, I'm going to cut your hair today."

Harlan shoots me a searing stare. "Thanks, man. Thanks a lot." His gaze drifts to my overnight bag. "You out of town again?"

"Off to Vegas for a couple nights. And then to New York straight from there."

"Ooh, can I water your plants while you're gone?" Abby offers as a red Nissan turns onto the block. My Spidey senses tingle—I have a feeling that's Sierra's Lyft.

I'll only be gone for five days, but Abby loves to take care of the pitching corps. "That would be fantastic. Can you do that on Wednesday? Is she with you on Wednesday?" I ask Harlan.

He nods. "Indeed she is. I have a game this weekend, so she'll be with her mom after that. But Wednesday is good."

I turn back to Abby. "You still have the door code from last time?"

She recites her personal code.

"Brilliant," I say, then tap her code into the Nest to activate it for the next week. "But don't polish their leaves."

She laughs. "You're so silly. I'd never do that."

"Thanks for helping out."

"I can't wait," she says with so much spirit she could run a cheer squad.

"Good luck with the hair and nails," I say as the Lyft slows to a stop. I turn my gaze to the woman in the back seat and a smile spreads on my face. *Hey there,* I mouth.

Harlan's eyes drift to the car, then to me. "Does Grant know you're seeing his sister?"

Talk about direct. A kernel of tension tightens in my gut. "Yes," I say, but that's not entirely true. "Mostly, I mean."

Harlan chuckles, scratching his chin. "Mostly isn't yes, my friend."

"Trust me, I know. But Grant's on vacay and . . ."

He nods a few times. "I hear ya. And hey, you like who you like. Just, maybe, tell him when you can."

That knot twists my stomach. "It's just a getaway trip. Nothing more."

With a doubtful expression, Harlan pats my shoulder. "Didn't look like just a getaway trip when you stared stupidly at her two seconds ago like you were falling for her," he says, then wheels around, picks up his daughter, and lifts her onto his shoulders. "And now, we're off to the store."

"Yay! It's a Daddy-back ride," Abby declares, then blows me a kiss as she's carried off.

I take a few seconds to collect my thoughts. To process that word he flung my way.

Falling.

Yes, I like Sierra. Yes, maybe I'm thinking about more than a fling. But falling? No way can that be happening so quickly.

Just no way.

I'm not that kind of guy. She's not that kind of woman. That just won't happen to us, no matter how stupidly I stare or how fast my heart hammers when I see her.

I slide into the back seat, kiss her soft cheek, and head to the airport.

* * *

Tight black jeans.

Short gray boots.

A slinky silver top that slopes off her shoulder.

Mmm. I am living my best life here in Vegas as I admire my date. I retrieve my credit card from the bill at the sushi joint as she returns from the restroom, gloss reapplied, her lips all pink and even more kissable.

"Stop being so distracting, woman. I can't concentrate on anything but you," I say as I fill in the tip amount then stand.

"Maybe I don't want you to concentrate on anything else," she says, stopping in front of me, then letting her fingers travel along the buttons of my shirt.

I clasp her hand and we leave the restaurant. "And now let's see Lulu."

"I can't wait to check her out. And I definitely want your opinion, okay?" Sierra asks, and it makes me happy, too, to be a part of her professional life. "I trust your judgement."

"We will do a thorough post-mortem," I say as we head through the concourse of The Extravagant, soundtracked by the cha-ching of slot machines, the clink of glasses, and the whir of the roulette wheel.

"Do you want to play later?" I ask.

"Slots? Blackjack? Poker?"

"Any of the above. Though, honestly, you don't strike me as a gambler," I say as we weave past the craps tables.

"I'm not really. You might have noticed—I'm *not* the most impulsive person," she says in a stage whisper.

"Yeah, I might have noticed. You like to take your time. Noodle on things. Contemplate them."

"That's me to a T." She lets out a long exhale then meets my gaze even as we walk. "That's why I waited so long to have sex."

I never asked why she'd waited. Asking would imply there was something wrong with her taking her time. Some people just wait. Sometimes you're not ready. Sometimes circumstances hold you back. Sometimes you simply don't meet the right person at the right time.

But I do want to know.

"You waited because you're not impulsive?" I ask.

"Yes, and that's because of my parents. They did what they wanted when they wanted. They didn't care about consequences. They had Grant when they were sixteen and me when they were eighteen, and they weren't interested in us," she says, matter-of-factly, but I bet it took her a long time to get to the place where she could be so direct about that.

"And your grandparents mostly raised you then? Grant's talked about them, introduced me to them. But I never knew the details."

"Our parents fought a ton when we were growing up. They were hotheaded and foul-mouthed. It was really hard on Grant since he's a couple years older, and he bore the brunt of it," she says as we walk past a man in a suit who shouts *Jackpot,* one fist in the air. Seems I'm not the only one getting lucky in Vegas.

We follow the signs for the comedy club as she shares: "They were so focused on their own things. My mom's a singer; Dad's a guitar player. They were interested in club gigs way more than raising us, so they were barely even around, but when they were around, they fought. We were afterthoughts."

That hurts my heart. I wish she hadn't gone through that pain. "I'm so sorry you had to deal with that," I say, squeezing her hand.

She squeezes back. "Thanks. But I'm lucky. My grandparents pretty much raised me, and I love them like crazy." Her soft smile spreads as her eyes flicker with happiness, perhaps inspired by memories of those two. "But still, I didn't want to be distracted from my goals. I wanted to go to college, do well, save money. So I put sex on the back burner until after I finished studying."

This speaks volumes about Sierra—her work ethic, her focus, hell, even her matching panties.

"You want to live life on your own terms," I say, as we reach the club. We stop outside the entrance, and I tug her into a quiet corner of the hallway to chat more. "And for sex, that meant you wanted to wait. Those were *your* terms."

Her shoulders seem to lighten, like she's relieved to share her reason. "I needed the right man, the right time. I wanted to be an adult. That's what I needed," she says, laying bare her wishes for me, and I love being let in so deeply. It's a rush to get to know her more. To hear what's going on in her mind.

"And how are you handling it?" I ask.

She shoots me a shy smile. "Pretty damn well," she says, then runs a hand down my shirt again. "I'm glad I waited. Glad I wasn't impulsive. But . . . that also means I kind of want to be that way this weekend. I've spent so many nights focused on the bar, building it to be one of the best in the city. I've been lasered in on work responsibilities and paying off loans. But now? On this trip? I kind of want to let loose and forget my bar baby. It's safe with Zoey babysitting, so I can go out and have all the fun. Gamble. Take chances. Dance, stay out late, play blackjack. I feel like I can be impulsive with you."

She sounds delighted with the prospect of doing it up in the city of sin, and hell, I am too. But what I like even more is that what she's really saying is that she trusts me. Proof that we can return to the way we were when Vegas ends. "Count me in for all that."

"I will," she promises, and we make our way to the club door.

A throat clears, and I turn. A young woman with lush brown hair and olive skin flashes me a tentative grin. "Excuse me. Are you Last Chance Train?" She squeezes her shoulders like she's on pins and needles for my answer.

"That's me," I say.

"Ah! I thought it might be you. I'm a huge Cougars fan, and I was at the ballpark when you threw the final pitch of the World Series last year. It was amazing." She presses her hand to her heart as if the memory lives there, then turns to Sierra. "Wasn't it?"

"It was incredible," Sierra agrees.

The woman bounces in her Converse sneakers. "Can I take a pic?"

"Of course," I say.

"Do you want me to take it?" Sierra offers.

"Oh my God, that would be amazing," she says. "By the way, I'm Bianca."

"Nice to meet you, Bianca," I say as I line up next to her.

Sierra snaps a picture. Bianca looks on the back of the camera, then thanks us before she practically skips down the hall.

My date shoots me an approving grin. "Look at you with your baller lifestyle, getting recognized and all."

That's the trouble, though.

I'm not wildly famous, but I'm known well enough that someone else might spot us, might take another picture.

A shot with a fan is one thing. But a candid snap of Sierra and me? Is that how I want Grant to find out I'm here with her?

Hell, no.

There are loopholes in the bro code, and then there's flagrant disregard, and I need to be on the right side of that line.

"I should tell Grant we're here. Just in case someone else sees us," I say.

Worry flickers in Sierra's eyes, then she nods. "Of course."

Once inside the club, we grab a table, and I tap out a note to Grant on my phone.

Chance: Hey. Just wanted you to know I'm hanging out with your sister in Vegas for a few days. We had a great time in Hawaii, so we're spending more time together.

I show it to her. "Straightforward," she says diplomatically.

Yeah, the text is direct. It covers the facts, not the feelings. But at least I've said something to my friend. I probably should say more, but not tonight.

I turn the phone on silent, slip it into my front pocket, and wrap my arm around Sierra's shoulder, pulling her close. "By the way, this is not hanging out. This is a helluva lot more."

She nestles closer, something like a shudder moving through her. "It is for me too, Chance."

We settle in and watch the show, enjoying the show, enjoying each other.

The trouble is, I'm pretty sure Harlan was dead right, and I have no clue what that means for the code, for my rules, and for the man I want to be.

All I know is this—I want to be with Sierra well beyond Las Vegas, whatever that may look like.

However that might play out.

24

SIERRA

I never knew how I'd feel about morning sex.

As the sun rises above the horizon, rosy light streaming through the window, Chance murmurs a sultry *good morning,* then tugs me against him.

In all of two seconds, I decide I very much want to find out if I like morning sex.

He pulls my back to his chest, peppers kisses all along my neck, and into my hair. Whispering sweet nothings like *beautiful, so soft, so gorgeous.*

"Love your hair and this sexy, pink strand," he whispers as he runs a finger along that colorful lock of my hair. "It's so very you."

I smile into his touches, enjoying that he's already figuring me out. But mostly enjoying the way he's touching me, those big, strong hands roaming up my stomach, making me shiver.

Chance cups my breasts, squeezing them, drawing out a long, low moan from my throat. He presses his body harder against me, his thick cock announcing its intentions right up against my ass.

I wiggle against his erection as a burst of lust swirls through me. "Mmm. I want you."

"Let me grab a condom," he says, reaching for one on the nightstand.

As he covers himself, my hand drifts down between my thighs, and I stroke. "I'm so turned on already," I whisper, and my God, it's freeing to say what I want to someone I trust. A man I want. A man I can share my fantasies with.

"Good. Me too," he rasps against my neck. "I'm turned on just from waking up next to you."

"Your kisses got me all worked up." I stroke a little faster, savoring the wetness—the slick, hot feel of already being this aroused.

Pushing my thigh up toward my chest, he rubs the head of his cock against my center.

I groan, closing my eyes, relishing the sleepy morning sexy times. He eases inside, and I gasp, thrilling at the feel of him, sliding inch by delicious inch into my body.

Once he's all the way there, he moves in slow, luxurious strokes, like we have all the time in the world. Like he wants to revel in my body. His hands travel everywhere, coasting up and down my skin, always returning to my breasts. "Grab them harder," I tell him, urging him on.

He growls against my neck, biting down on my skin as he grips my breasts. "Like that?"

"Yes. Just like that."

He squeezes while he rocks into me. “I want it all with you. I just do.”

I want it all with him too.

More than sex.

More than these nights in Las Vegas.

Seconds later, we come together. It’s rough and passionate, and then, he’s soft and tender as he kisses my shoulder, murmuring, “You’re incredible. You’ve gone to my head, Sierra.” His voice is stripped bare and vulnerable, and I feel like we’re both tiptoeing closer to a brand-new reality. One that scares the hell out of me and maybe him too.

What if this thing between us is becoming the very thing we both sought to avoid?

* * *

The rest of the day, we indulge.

We play poker, we go to a magic show, we buy chocolate-covered strawberries, and we play slots.

Late in the afternoon, while we’re parked at an *Aladdin* machine, Chance’s phone vibrates in his pocket. He takes it out, squints, then winces. “It’s Grant.”

“Go ahead. Read it,” I say, hoping that whatever Grant writes isn’t going to make Chance withdraw, or worry we’re doing something wrong.

I’ve known all along that my brother’s not the real issue, but the code is for Chance, and Grant’s connected to that.

Chance shows me the message.

Grant: Thanks for the heads up. You better be good to her. That is all I have to say.

It's permission, in a way. Maybe an acknowledgment that this trip doesn't violate the code. "So how does that make you feel?"

Chance mulls it over, letting go of a long breath and some of the tension that crept in when he saw Grant had replied. "Better. I feel like as long as I'm good to you, I can have the things I'm looking for."

"You are good to me," I reassure him.

But will I still think that when this ends? When our deadline expires tomorrow morning? When he goes to New York and I head home to The Spotted Zebra?

I don't think he's bad news, or that he'll treat me badly. But I do fear the end of us could be hard on me. That letting him in so deeply brings so many risks, no matter how good he is.

"Why is the code so important to you?"

He inhales deep, contemplating the question. "Why do I love baseball?" he muses. "Why do I talk to plants? That's just who I am. I'm a guy who believes in rules and the benefits of them. I want people to be happy. I've always been that way, and after my parents split, I probably became even more like that. At the wedding, TJ pointed out that I was always the guy who tried to make sure everyone got along."

That sounds exactly like Chance. Grant told me how, back when he joined the team, Chance had been one of the first guys to truly welcome him to the Cougars.

"I don't think that's a bad thing," I say. "I've also noticed TJ has a lot of opinions. At the wedding, he told *me* not to break your heart." I put that out there to gauge how Chance might react to the idea of his heart being at stake.

His lips curve into a grin. "Is that so? He gave you the big brother warning?"

"Oh, yes. He sure did."

Chance swallows roughly, then tugs me closer. "I'd like to second that. Don't break my heart, Sierra," he whispers, his voice tight with emotion.

Whoa.

I wasn't expecting that. Maybe this is a new stage of the code—saying without words that we both want more. That we're going to give dating a shot beyond Vegas.

"I promise," I say.

It feels like we're in a cocoon of bliss, of possibilities. Possibilities that I desperately want.

* * *

That evening, we go to The Cosmopolitan to see the bartender I wanted to check out. Her bar tricks are movie-level amazing, with breathtaking long-pours and bottle-flips. It's impossible to look away.

But enjoying her drinks?

The opposite of impossible. They're as good as her tricks and as strong as her talent.

After a couple of cocktails, my head buzzes. My skin tingles. Everything feels warm and fantastic.

The world is gleaming silver and gold, and Chance and I can't stop touching and kissing and drinking.

When we leave the bar, he gestures to a sign for a night club. "In the mood to dirty dance?"

"Always."

In the club, we order more drinks, under the smoky haze and purple lights, we grind against each other, letting loose to the music.

As I float on the high of this night, I feel a million miles away from work and responsibilities. I'm breaking all the rules, shedding the last year of workaholism, and it's spectacular.

It's freedom and sensuality.

It's indulgence.

In the middle of a particularly dirty bump and grind, while the club is pulsing and we are swaying, a woman and a man rush to the center of the dance floor. The couple sports *Just Married* T-shirts, and they thrust their hands into the air, wild glee in their eyes.

I look at Chance, wiggle an eyebrow.

"That's so very impulsive," he says, nodding at their shirts.

"So very Vegas," I second.

He leans closer, shouting in my ear. "What Vegas trip is complete without a spontaneous wedding?"

None.

That sounds wicked. Thrilling. And utterly out of character.

"It's a must-do," I shout.

He locks eyes with me, his dark and hooded, more intense than they've ever been. "Let's get married."

25

CHANCE

That's what this adventure is all about—fun.

Letting go.

Saying yes.

Sierra and I make a fast exit for the car line at the front of the hotel. This is the best idea ever. It's so good it's bad, because I'm not a good guy. I'm a bad one.

I've had enough of codes, enough of coloring within the lines.

I'm done with them for tonight. I want to throw out the good guy rules in spectacular style.

We step out into the Nevada night, and I shout, "Screw the code." Even in Vegas, I'm noticeably loud. People spin and stare, eyes roaming over us.

I bring my finger to my lips. "Oops." I say, then tiptoe over-dramatically to the car service I ordered, Sierra laughing as we go.

We slide into the vehicle holding each other up, holding our sides. But the laughing stops once we leave the hotel. We make out the whole way to the Las Vegas Marriage License office.

* * *

Two hours later, we stumble through our hotel lobby, holding hands, wearing our *Just Married* sashes and matching rings glinting on our fingers. We pass crowds of guests, including the friendly woman from last night.

"Bianca! We're married," I call out to her as she wanders past an *Avengers* slot machine.

Sierra waggles the flowers as evidence. "Mr. and Mrs!"

"Eeek! Yay! I love weddings! Congrats," the brunette says, then throws her arms around both of us and hugs hard.

We say goodbye and make our way up the elevator then down our hall. I scoop Sierra up, carry her over the threshold and kick the door closed.

The lust that's been running hot all night hits a new level.

I bring her to the bed and drop her onto the mattress, ready to have her. Seconds later, we're stripped down to nothing.

I push her knees wide open and bury my face in the paradise between her thighs, kissing and licking and working her over till she's begging for me inside her.

"Please, Chance. Now."

I rise and grab a condom, suiting up. "Get those sexy legs over my shoulders because I want to fuck my wife hard on the bed."

She does as I ask, and soon, I'm sliding home. Once I'm there, I'm sure coming to Vegas with her was the craziest decision I've made, at least recently, but maybe the best one too.

I lower my chest to hers, and we find just the right rhythm.

She moans and I groan, and we move in tandem. Her fingers play with my hair. "God, it's so good with you. Everything feels so good with you," she murmurs.

Those words—all of them—hook into my heart. They dig into my mind. They make me feel incredible.

And I want to feel connected too.

No—even more connected. I slow down, look into her eyes, and the enormity of the moment crashes over me.

I'm sleeping with my wife.

And everything feels right.

I wrap my arms under and around her shoulders.

"Chance," she whispers. It sounds full of all sorts of beauty and wonder. "I'm falling for you."

A dam breaks somewhere inside me. I'm so relieved she said it first. So glad I can say it too.

"Oh, Sierra, I'm already there," I reply, and then I bury my face in her neck as we come together, all limbs and sweat and promises made in the city of sin after midnight.

26

CHANCE

Sunlight streams cruelly through the windows.

A sledgehammer hits my head.

Not just once, but over and over.

I blink my eyes as far open as a squint.

I haven't seen the inside of a hangover in years, and I'm seeing the inside, outside and upside-down of one right now.

An obnoxious ring blares from my phone.

Again.

And again.

Fumbling for it, I find it on the nightstand and hit snooze.

Sierra doesn't rustle.

I trudge to the bathroom, hunt for some ibuprofen, down them, and return to bed.

Curling up next to Sierra, I conk out for another twenty minutes.

* * *

The alarm blasts again.

Loud.

Insistent.

What time is it?

"Oh crap." Sierra's worry registers, and I push up on my elbows, yawning.

"What's wrong?" I ask, catching a glimpse of gold on my finger.

Oh.

Right.

Yup.

We had the bright idea last night to get hitched.

Which was crazy, but hell, did it feel good at the time.

I think?

I scratch my head. Everything feels fuzzy.

"Your flight. It leaves in an hour and twenty. Mine leaves in an hour and ten. Shit, shit, shit!" She flies out of bed, naked as the day she was born.

She slams the bathroom door shut, and seconds later, the faucet is running.

The sound of furious teeth brushing accompanies me as I jump out of bed, hoof it to my bag for some boxer briefs, and quickly get dressed.

Two minutes later, Sierra swings open the door. "We need to go ASAP."

"I know," I say, as my head pounds again, and I groan in frustration.

"I'm annoyed too," she mutters as she grabs her clothes from the bed, wheeling around to snag more from the floor.

"That annoyed voice was for my . . . headache. It's like a murder went down in my brain," I say as I head to the bathroom with my bag.

"I think my brain was an accessory to the crime. Maybe an alibi," she says, stuffing shoes into her bag.

Checking the time again, I speed-brush my teeth, scoop all my toiletries into my arms and dump them in my carry-on. I grab some ibuprofen and pour a glass of water, then bring it to her. "Here. This should help. My headache is a little better already."

Her shoulders relax as she pops the pills in her mouth then swallows them. "Thanks," she says, and she sets the cup on the bureau.

I scan the room for stray belongings and grab my watch from the nightstand, along with my phone charger. As Sierra stuffs her feet into flats, I dump everything into my bag, stopping when I find the *Just Married* sashes poking out from under the bed.

What do I do with these? They're hardly a souvenir.

But I can't bring myself to toss them, so I stuff them into my suitcase.

"I'll call a Lyft," I say, entering the info in my app.

Fifteen minutes after we get up, we rush out of the suite, Mr. and Mrs. I Have No Fucking Clue What Is Happening.

In the elevator, I turn to face her. "So . . ."

"Yeah . . . so." She gazes down at her hand, staring at it like her ring-finger has turned blue.

"I guess we got married last night," I say, heavily.

What the hell kind of insane idea was that? Caught

up in the night and the feelings, that's what I came up with? A Vegas wedding?

How about: *I'm falling in love with you. Let's stay together and date.*

Instead, I blurted out *let's get married* because that's . . . fun?

I should have turned to Google.

To TJ.

To my own brain.

Instead, I went with my drunken heart.

Sierra sighs too, raising her left hand. "I guess we did."

The elevator arrives at the ground floor with a *ding*.

Vegas is an empty stage in the morning—lights up, artifice exposed. The magic of the neon nights vanishes at dawn. What's left is overturned glasses, big bets lost, and decisions bathed in regret.

I steal a glance at Sierra. Does she regret last night? "So, um," I begin, my throat raspy from the shouting at the club. "Do we just get . . ." I break away, barely able to voice the words. But I have to say them. ". . . an annulment?"

She winces like the thought causes physical pain. She lifts her hand to her head, sets her palm on her forehead, and lets out a low, plaintive moan.

"Your head still hurts?"

She nods, cringing like she's trying to fight off the pain.

"We can talk about this another time," I say gently.

But can we? And when? What the hell do we do to fix this? To undo this?

Once we're at the entrance, I spot our Lyft quickly. I set our bags in the trunk before the driver can and slide inside.

"Airport, right?"

"Yup," I say as I buckle in and Sierra does the same.

She lifts her face, sighs. "Yes to the annulment," she says, returning to the issue. "I mean, that seems the simplest. Maybe the airport has a booth for annulments?"

I laugh humorlessly. "They have slot machines. Seems they ought to have quickie divorce options."

Divorce.

That word tastes like spoiled milk.

"They definitely should." She looks down at her phone. "It'll be close, but we should make it."

"Good, good." I don't know what else to say.

Hey, let's not get annulled.

Let's go out on more dates.

I search for annulments at the airport but come up empty. "I guess they don't offer—"

She interrupts with a muttered, "Oh God."

"What's wrong now?"

Brandishing her phone, she shows me a picture.

A photo of us with our *Just Married* sashes on.

Dread coils in me. If she's got that picture, everyone does. That means everyone's going to know I broke the rules. I violated the code. I'm *not* a good guy.

"Where's that from?" I ask nervously.

"Clementine sent it to me. She said, *Congratulations, you little stinker. Next time I want to be there*. Said she saw it on Insta. And here's another one, from my friend

Erin. *Omg that is so epic.* And my brother. *Something you want to tell me?"*

With a groan, I click open my phone, and like Sierra's, my texts light up.

Shane: You sneaky, cheeky fucker! Congrats!

Harlan: Guess you did realize you were falling after all!

TJ: Details. Now.

Grant: I go away to Hawaii, you pretend to date my sister, take her to Vegas, and then get married. Okayyyy!????

One more click over to Instagram confirms that Bianca tagged us in a photo at the hotel last night. I don't even remember her taking one. But clearly, I don't recall a lot of last night.

I meet Sierra's gaze and shrug helplessly. "I guess we were impulsive last night," I say in the biggest of understatements.

"Just a little bit." Her tone is strained.

A few minutes later, the car pulls up at the airport. There's no time to dwell on our next step, though—a quick ride up the escalator reveals a long line at security.

"TSA pre-check," Sierra says, pointing and race walking.

That line isn't short either. But after fifteen minutes

of raw nerves and *c'mons* muttered under my breath, we make it to the other side.

My phone flashes with an alert that my flight to New York is boarding now.

She shows me hers. Her flight is already boarding group C.

"I need to go," she says, sounding as lost as I feel.

I part my lips, but no words come.

My head is a mess, a scattered jumble of nonsense.

Saying "Let's get divorced and date," sounds dumb. Saying "Let's stay married but just date," sounds even dumber.

That's ridiculous.

Completely and utterly ridiculous.

I lean in, dust a kiss onto her cheek, then say, "I'll take care of this, I promise."

When we break apart, her brow is knit with worry. "Take care of this?"

I flap a hand in the direction of the city. "You know. Last night." Tension winds in me like a too-tight instrument. "I meant everything. I'm crazy about you, but I need to go."

"Me too," she says, wistful.

I turn and run down the concourse, swipe my boarding pass at the gate, then step onto the jetway.

I turn around for one last look, like this is a movie and she'll run after me. Or I'd rush after her instead, calling, "Wait, I made a terrible mistake," planting a tender kiss on her lips when I reach her.

Then I'd tell her I'm in love with her.

But this isn't a movie—this is the real world.

And the reality is, I fucked up.

Badly.

27

SIERRA

"And it all happened so quickly!"

The petite brunette at the bar chirps as she flips her hand back and forth. I'm surprised she can lift it at all, what with the weight of the robin's egg on her finger. "He asked me to marry him after only a month!"

She snuggles up against her fiancé, a strapping lumberjack type as he flashes a grin. "When you know, you know."

I shoot them a practiced smile as I slide over their margaritas. "Congratulations. That's so wonderful. And truly, I'm honored that you met here."

She coos, stroking the bar. "I love The Spotted Zebra so much. This is our special place, isn't it, baby?"

He runs a thumb along her jaw. "Always, honey."

They're too much. Too perfect. Too in love.

But they're also proof—one month is fast.

One week, then, is crazy.

Which makes five nights *certifiable.*

What was I thinking? I seriously can't believe I did that—got married in Vegas. That was just so . . . *not me.*

So out of character.

And yet, I'm so freaking blue listening to this happy couple toast their love and my bar.

"To The Spotted Zebra! All great loves begin here," the brunette says.

I laugh to cover up the bubble of sadness threatening to burst inside me, and I glance around. This place has always cheered me up. It's like my kid, making me feel proud and happy at the same time. The bar is the reason I didn't want to get serious. Hell, it's the reason I felt so dumb the other morning for getting married on a whim.

But as I look around at the busy joint—it's jumping—all I see are the spots where Chance and I began.

Right here at the counter, a year ago, when we chatted and I felt those first sparks.

Then back in April, he came here with the guys but spent the whole evening talking to me.

Another visit, over the summer, he stayed late and we played a game of pool.

What did we discuss?

Music, TV, our families, our days.

It's always just been so easy with Chance. Everything clicked.

And now, when I survey my home away from home, a new thought occurs to me.

This—Chance and me—didn't happen in five days.

It happened slowly, day by day, night by night.

And damn it, I should have been responsible. Should

have just told him I wanted to, well, date like normal adults. Instead, we both went crazy and flew straight at the sun in one wild moment.

The result? We burned too brightly, turning into ash.

I stare down at my hand, my naked finger.

My ring is at home.

All alone.

I take a deep breath, force away the regrets, and slap on a smile for the next round of customers.

* * *

When I return to my place, I slump onto the couch. Tom struts across the floor and hops up to join me.

"Meow?"

He's asking if I'm okay.

"I don't know. Yes. No. Maybe?" I answer, then I reach for the gold band I left on the coffee table. Tom parks himself on my lap, stretching out and purring.

I turn the ring over in my fingers, like it holds vital answers. But to what questions? Was it crazy to get married? Were we fools? Was Chance falling in love with me too? Or was what we said after we tied the knot all smoke and mirrors?

Was anything real?

I've no idea.

I rub my thumb over the ring. It's just a piece of metal, meaningless now.

Chance will *take care of it* and end our joke of a marriage.

My phone buzzes, and I click open my texts, hoping

it's him. But of course, it's three in the morning in Manhattan.

Clementine: Are you okay? Do you want some violet and sage leaf candles? I have a new face mask that's incredible. Or . . . wine! How about flowers? I picked up some pretty lilies from Frankie's. I can come over!

Sierra: It's after midnight, but thank you.

Clementine: Breakfast, then? Let me cheer you up. It's my special skill.

I smile half-heartedly. It *is* her skill. She's amazingly happy. And I could use some of that.

I say yes, then I curl up with Tom, wrapping my arms around my cat therapist.

"I just miss Chance, and I feel so stupid," I tell him, my voice wobbly. "And I think I fucked everything up."

Tom sets a paw on my chest.

He understands me completely.

28

CHANCE

I have a new twenty-thousand-dollar watch.

Yay.

And my agent just re-upped me with Victoire and told me *my wife's* matching watch is in the mail, and that it'd have been with me sooner, but she had no idea I was getting married.

Point taken, loud and clear.

As I head to meet Shane for lunch in Gramercy Park, the same sense of what-the-hell-do-I-do hangs over me like a cloud of bad cologne.

I stride down Park Avenue, trying to savor November in New York City. I've always loved Manhattan, from its energy to its take-no-prisoners vibe. From the plethora of food, to the panoply of people, this city gives me life.

This afternoon, though?

I feel . . . regret. For days, it's been swirling in my gut like thick tar, weighing me down.

When I reach the sushi bar, I try to shuck off the feeling.

Don't be a Doug Downer.

Inside, my British friend has already claimed a spot at the bar, and he raises a hand to get my attention. When I reach him, Shane stands, claps me on the back. "How's it going, mate?"

"Great," I say, mustering enthusiasm I don't have. Happiness I haven't located since I messed up royally in the land of big eff-ups.

But I should find some energy. Friends are important. Showing up for them matters. Shane said he has news, so I need to get in the supportive friend zone.

"This place has the best unagi," he says. "And the scallops will make you want to marry them."

I shudder.

He chuckles. "Did you have a row with scallops once upon a time?"

"No. Sorry. Gut reaction."

"Ah. The marriage thing." He smacks my shoulder. "But you should be happy now. The ex is in the rearview mirror, and you've got a lovely new bride. Cheers, mate. We need to celebrate."

The regret sinks deeper in my stomach.

But what the hell do I regret, exactly? Marrying Sierra? Or is it how I bungled the morning after?

Or maybe, it's everything.

Every damn thing I did wrong.

Like going about falling in love backward.

But there's no time to ponder my epic fail any more than I already have—that is, for nearly every waking second since I left Las Vegas—because a waitress arrives and asks if we'd like a drink.

Shane orders a sake, so when in Rome . . .

When the server leaves, Shane arches a brow. "So, marriage. Is it all that the second time around? You seem much happier, judging from that photo."

I wince, scrub a hand across my jaw. "It's . . . complicated."

Shane takes a beat, his brow furrowing, then he seems to put two and two together. "Oh, you're getting a divorce? It was one of those pissed-in-Vegas-marriage-lark moments, and now you've seen the light of day?"

That sounds awful too. "Sort of. I don't know."

"This does sound complicated. What's the story?" He wiggles his fingers. "Serve it up to Shakespeare."

Sighing, I slump back in the chair, rub my palm across the back of my neck. I'm tired of keeping all this inside. TJ's been out of town and just returned today, so I won't see him till later this afternoon. It'll be good to get this mess of feelings off my chest. "Let's see. She and I went to my cousin's wedding as fake dates, leveled-up to real dating, took a spontaneous trip to Vegas, then got married after five days of real/fake dating, but she never wanted a serious relationship and I didn't think I did either. And now we're married and need to get divorced. Also, everything sucks."

It's a relief to say that out loud after wearing my *everything-is-fantastic* smile around sponsors for the last two days.

Shane takes a deep breath. "That's a little crazy. I'll grant you that."

"Yup."

The waitress returns with our sakes and I thank her. We order sushi, and when she leaves, I take a drink.

It tastes horrid.

It reminds me of my hangover. I'm never drinking again—add that to my list of regrets. So much for all my rules on how to behave. *Don't get skunk-faced drunk and post pictures on social.*

Well, I *didn't* post the pic. But that's little consolation.

"But," Shane adds, "I have one little question."

I try to shove off the personal pity party I'm throwing in my head. "Yeah? What's that?"

He clears his throat. "You said she never wanted a serious relationship and you *didn't think* you did either." He takes a beat. "But do you now?"

There's no question. "I do."

"Then start with that as you try to solve *this* problem. Maybe see if she does now too," he says.

"See if she wants a relationship?"

"Yes. That."

It's so simple.

And it's not a bad idea. In fact, it's an excellent one. But *how* is the question.

I'll noodle on it today. Grateful to focus on someone else, I rap my knuckles on the bar. "Tell me your news."

He grins. "There's a good chance you'll be seeing more of me in San Francisco. My agent is in talks with the Dragons about a potential trade. I miss California, so cross your fingers it'll go through."

"Holy shit! That'd be awesome, man. So the city would have the best closer in the game in me, and . . . someone sort of decent . . . in you," I say with a wicked smile.

"You're such a delight, Chance. I'm so glad I gave you romance advice. You can fuck off with it now," he says, laughing.

"I hope it comes through. It'll be good to see you around, Shakespeare," I add.

And I mean it.

Friends in the same field are golden. That's why I need to make good with Grant. Make sure I haven't fucked things up too badly.

When lunch is over, I say goodbye and head to meet TJ. All the way there, I cogitate on an idea that has taken hold of my brain—a plan that could fix this whole situation.

At least, that's my hope.

* * *

"That's your plan?" my brother asks, arching a skeptical brow after I give him the details.

"Well, yeah."

TJ shakes his head as he gathers an iced tea for me and a coffee for himself at Doctor Insomnia's on Columbus Avenue. "Wrong."

"Why is that wrong?"

"You're in love with Sierra. Right?" he asks as we head to a table.

"Yes, like you kinda guessed at the wedding."

"So, your plan is to just return to the city, see Grant and tell him, then go to The Spotted Zebra to see her." He recaps like he wants to make sure he understood exactly what I just said.

But my plan seemed reasonable enough to me. Practical. "Yes."

He hums doubtfully and takes a swallow of his coffee. "And . . . what then? Because that's a terrible idea."

Bristling, I lift my mug, take a drink. "I don't know why you think it's such a bad idea. It's practical, like a plan should be."

Rolling his eyes, he laughs. "Chance, little brother. You're looking at this the wrong way. You fucked up badly. It's not time for a *practical* plan. It's big gesture time. With *the* woman. Go big or go home."

I wince, that regret turning into a tornado inside me again. "So that means?"

TJ stares at me, like he's waiting for me to figure out the answer. "Time to own it."

I let his words echo and expand in my head.

Own it.

Own my feelings.

Own my choices.

And own my trouble.

In a flash, I see a different ending to our story.

I've been looking at the problem in the wrong light.

Just like when I'm on the mound—there's more than one pitch to get you out of a jam.

Some sticky situations call for a blazing fastball. Others require a cutter. Now and then, you need a changeup.

The best closers in the game don't rely on only one pitch to solve a bases-loaded quandary.

I've been throwing the wrong stuff at my bro code. No wonder it blew up spectacularly in Vegas.

Now, I need a better game plan, starting with my catcher.

I smile for the first time since I woke up married to the woman I love.

29

CHANCE

Back at my hotel, I call Grant on video. This is an in-person convo, but it can't wait, so FaceTime will have to do.

Grant answers after a couple rings, his face appearing on the screen, his hair a mess. He's in his living room, stretched out on his couch. A pair of feet rests on his thighs, just at the edge of the screen. Declan's feet.

"Hey. What's up . . . brother-in-law?" Grant asks, a little wary, but still his usual affable self.

"Hey, Grant. Hello, Declan's feet."

"Hi, Chance," Declan says from off-camera. "Proceed."

I laugh nervously. "Thanks. I guess you guys know what this is about?"

Grant scratches his chin. "I'm not really a mind reader. But I suspect it's about what went down in Vegas?"

No time to waste. I dive in, taking TJ's advice,

owning it. "Listen. I feel like a jackass. I know I violated the golden rule—don't hook up with a teammate's sister."

Declan laughs. "Is that a rule?"

Grant looks at his guy. "Not for you, sweetheart." Then he turns back to me. "Okay. I mean, I'm not sure that's a rule per se. But go on."

"It's a rule I *wanted* to follow," I say, emphasis on the past tense. I take a soldiering breath. "I *didn't* want to create problems with the team or the chemistry or anything like that. And that's why I avoided the reality that I've been falling for your sister over the last year. I didn't want conflicts, or for anything to be awkward."

Grant nods.

"And the thing is, I'm done with that."

"You are?" he asks carefully.

This is what I learned tonight when all the lights went on in my head. It's crystal clear now what has been holding me back.

Me.

My rigid adherence to a code.

But some rules need to be bent. Some need to be broken. And some, you just have to let go of entirely.

I'm done with getting in my own way.

Goodbye, code. Hello, life.

"I was focused on the wrong thing," I tell Grant, feeling lighter already, like I'm shucking off the regret that stymied me the last few days. "I was worried about the team. I didn't want to rock the boat. But you know what was happening?"

Grant chuckles softly, shaking his head. "No, clue me in."

Declan pops into view. "I kinda want to hear this too."

I can't believe I'm about to say something so damn obvious. I should have it emblazoned on a T-shirt. "It was never about you," I tell Grant.

Grant wags a finger at me as he smiles. "Aha, Sherlock. You figured it out."

"I was using you as an excuse because I was terrified of getting involved again. Of seeing my life dragged through the online mud again. Of getting hurt. Of everything." I serve up all my fears on a silver platter. And I *own them*, finally, which means, I hope, that I can change what I do about them. "I didn't realize I was doing it, but I held tight to that code. Clutched it like I was dangling from the windowsill of a thirty-story building and I didn't want to die. But I learned something today."

"Go on," Grant says, enthused.

"You were never the problem. I was. I was afraid of falling in love, of wanting to be with someone. Of caring about someone so much I might get my heart broken again." I swallow roughly as emotions rise in me. "And I'm done with being afraid."

"Sounds a lot like the real thing," he says, and his arm shifts, maybe to hold hands with Declan.

"It is."

Grant turns to Declan. "Am I the relationship oracle today, or what?"

Declan laughs. "Seems so."

I tilt my head. "What does that mean?"

"Don't worry about that. So, what next?" Grant asks.

It's a good question. But I'm pretty sure I know the answer.

And it lies in San Francisco.

30

SIERRA

A little earlier that same day

Clementine arrives in the morning with a knock and a bright *ding-dong*.

I swing open the door, invite her in. She carries a pink box on her palm, like a waiter in a fancy restaurant. "Breakfast, aka cupcakes."

"The breakfast of champions," I say as we head to the kitchen. She's so cheery, I refuse to stay in my funk.

She sets the box down on the counter, then slides a canvas bag off her shoulder, reaching in to extract a bouquet of lilies.

"As promised," she says.

Grabbing a vase from a shelf, I fill it with water and pop in the flowers. "Gorgeous," I declare.

"See? Flowers make everything a little better," she says.

I have a flash of a memory of me as a little girl, traipsing through a field of flowers.

Huh.

I always thought I loved flowers as an adult because they were lovely. But maybe I've always known they make a day better. I needed that when I was younger.

Maybe my love of flowers as a woman has never been about pretty little things, but more about necessary things. About the happy things we find when we're kids to get us through tough times. Through days when we don't feel loved and wanted.

I sought that out in the world, looking for it in beauty, but I found it in other places too—my grandparents, my brother, my friends.

Myself.

I have all that now and more.

Friends, a cat, a business I adore. And today, sweets.

Clementine gestures to the box. "Chocolate buttercream or vanilla dream?"

I scoff. "Is that a trick question? Both. We split them."

She smiles brightly. "Perfect answer."

We break the cupcakes in half, and I stuff a bite of the vanilla in my mouth. "Mmm. This is delish," I say after I chew.

"Best therapy ever," she says once she's done. Then her smile disappears. "Spill. You fell in love and are afraid to tell him, right?"

Whoa. Someone doesn't mince words. I gulp then head for the fridge and pour a glass of milk. I down it, then face the music.

"Yes. That's true," I admit.

She nods sympathetically. "It's your armor, girl. That's what's holding you back. The question is—are you going to let it?"

It's an excellent question.

Am I ready to go after more than friends, a cat, a business I adore, and sweets?

* * *

Tom follows me around all that morning, alternating between meowing and purring.

The cat seems determined to tell me something. As I dress for work, he rubs against my leg, kicking up his motor to another level entirely. I've never heard him this loud.

I bend down. "What is it, love?"

He answers with more purring then stretches his front legs along my calves. I scoop him into my arms. "Did you just want to snuggle?"

The cat rubs his head against me. I laugh. "I swear, all you ever want is . . ."

I break off, startled by the obvious.

He's a love bug.

He just wants love.

Maybe he has the right idea.

Am I going to take love advice from a cat?

Well, first I have to head into work to open for an early happy hour. But along the way, I text Grant and make a request.

* * *

I unlock the door to The Spotted Zebra. We open in an hour and a half, but I've mastered doing the prep work in less than sixty minutes. I bust my butt in a flurry of activity, readying the place I love for another night.

Last night, I felt so disconnected from my bar baby. Today, I'm connected again, and it feels so good.

The breakfast with Clementine reset me. The message from the cat perhaps did too. I'm pretty sure it's time to woman up and rip off my armor, but I want to talk to someone else first.

Before we open, Grant strolls in.

"To what do you owe the honor of my presence?" he asks, then I blink.

I point.

Gawk.

My jaw hits the floor. "Is that a . . .?"

I can't even finish.

He flashes his left hand at me, grinning. "Oh, this?"

"Yes," I blurt out, flustered. "Is that a band? An engagement ring?"

His grin takes over the city. "Why, yes. I did get engaged in Hawaii."

My hand flies to my mouth and tears rain down my cheeks. They don't stop as I run to my brother, fling my arms around him, and cry the happiest tears I've ever cried. It took him five years and a lot of heartbreak to find his way back to Declan.

But he's here, on the other side of heartache.

On *this* side of love.

And I'm not sure I have any more questions. "I am so happy for you," I say in a broken voice—but from joy, not from pain.

"Thanks. Me too," he says, brimming with cheer. "Now, what about you? What the hell is going on? What do you need? You seemed distraught when you texted."

I swipe my tears away. "I was for a while. I was all mixed up about Mom and Dad, and the way I've tried to live differently from them," I say, my breath steadying into place again after the excitement. "But . . ." I shrug, letting go of all that in one fell swoop. It's time to say goodbye to the past. None of those issues seem to matter anymore. "You're engaged. You're happy. You didn't let them hold you back. And I shouldn't let them hold me back either."

He laughs and spreads his hands out wide. "Check me out. I walk into a bar, and I don't even have to say anything. I'm an instant problem solver."

"You are," I say, but truly, love is the problem solver.

* * *

Later, I slip out to run an errand, and at the end of the night, I send Chance a text.

Sierra: Miss you! Want to come over when you return tomorrow night? I would love to see you.

Well after midnight there's a knock on my door.

31

SIERRA

Always wear pretty panties if a man calls late at night.

Sounds like a good rule.

I'm wearing basic pink cotton underthings and a cami because I'm *not* expecting anyone.

Fear prickles down my spine, but I act quickly.

I grab the baseball bat I keep under my bed, snag my phone from the nightstand, and swing my legs out from under the sheets.

Just as I'm poised to dial 911, because who the fuck knocks at this hour, my phone beeps with a call.

"Oh!"

It's Chance.

I answer with a whisper. "Hello?"

"It's me. At your door. I'm a day early. Will you let me in?"

He's supposed to be in New York. But he's here. A thrill rushes through me. *He's here!*

"Yes, of course," I say, keeping the phone pressed to

my ear as I walk to the door, peer through the peephole, and nearly fly through the roof with excitement.

What is happening to me?

I've prided myself on being cool and collected. On being a badass babe. And I am positively giddy at the sight of the man who wants to divorce me.

But maybe he doesn't want to end us?

"Hi. I'll let you in," I say.

He smiles like a loon. A loon I love. "Thanks. I'll be right here," he teases.

I end the call, unlock the door, and yank it open.

"Hey," he says, soft and tender, then his brow knits as he points at the bat in my hand. "Don't get me wrong. You holding a baseball bat is insanely sexy, but do you want to put it down?"

I didn't realize I was still clutching it. I set it against the wall and open the door wider. "Come in," I say, and though I have no idea why he's here, I have a feeling that a visit after midnight is a good thing.

I shut the door, and he steps inside, determination in his deep brown eyes as he meets my gaze. "I love you, Sierra Blackwood. And the only thing I want to take care of is finding a way to stay together."

My breath catches.

I can't believe what he said.

It's exactly what I feel.

I step closer, cup his cheeks. "I love you too," I tell him, holding his face, my voice trembling.

When did I become such an emotional gal?

Oh, right. Maybe when I learned to embrace happiness as it comes. Something I'm learning literally this second.

"You do?" he asks, laughing incredulously, but joyfully too.

"I do," I say, giddy like my veins are filled with starlight and my heart contains the whole entire sky. "I started to fall for you in Hawaii, and I went head over heels in love in Vegas. And I want to date you. I want to stay with you. I want to be impulsive with you, and to be in love with you."

His lips twitch in a delicious smile, then he brings me close for a kiss I feel in my toes. I zing everywhere.

When he breaks the kiss, he nibbles on the corner of his lips, then says, "Let's be impulsive."

Then, he drops to one knee.

I gasp.

He reaches into his pocket, takes out a jewelry box, and flips it open.

"Oh my God," I whisper, awed. Utterly awed.

The diamond is an enchanting emerald-cut I never imagined he'd give me tonight.

Chance meets my gaze, vulnerability flickering in his eyes. "How about a replay on the Mr. and Mrs.? I want to be with you, and that means asking for your hand properly. I'm in love with you, and maybe it seems like it happened in five days, and maybe it did," he says, emotion threaded through every word. "But I think it's been happening for the last year, every time we saw each other. At least, that's how it's been for me, almost like we were dating without knowing we were dating.

And I don't want a halfway relationship with you," he adds, his voice strong. "I want it all, and I truly hope you do too."

I can't help it.

This non-crier cries again. Tears well and fall as I kneel in front of him, clasping his handsome face. "I want to be with you. It's the same for me, Chance. I've been falling in love with you for the last year too, just getting to know you. And I want to keep loving you."

"I do love you. So much," he whispers, then hauls me in for another kiss before he laughs, a little embarrassed.

"What is it?"

"I need to put this ring on you, and *then* I can get lost in kissing you," he says, and I hold out my hand.

He slides it on.

And wow.

Just wow.

I'm engaged to be married to my husband, and that sounds crazy, but it feels totally right and absolutely wonderful.

"I love it," I say, staring at the thing of beauty, then dipping my head, hiding my face. "And that makes my gift look pretty silly."

"You got me a gift?" He sounds utterly delighted.

"I did." I rise and head to the kitchen. He joins me and I reach for a tiny plant. "It's a zebra cactus for your plant collection. I texted you because I wanted to see you when you returned tomorrow and tell you I love you and give you a plant."

I hand him the little green thing.

He coos at it. "Awww. I love it. Can I call it Sierra?"

Scrunching my brow, I shake my head. "No way. How about we name it . . . Jordy?"

Chance cracks up. "I suppose he did sort of play a part in us getting together. And this plant is not silly. It's awesome. And I love it. And I love you."

This is all too wonderful, but I'm dying to know something. "What happened? What changed for you? I thought your code and the team and my brother and all that was the issue."

"It was, but then it wasn't." He sets the plant on the counter, his expression turning serious. "I realized that I'd been wrong. I thought your brother was the obstacle. But *I* was the problem. I was afraid of getting hurt, and I used the code as an excuse."

"Don't be afraid with me," I say gently. "I won't hurt you. After all, I told TJ I won't break your heart, and I meant it."

"I won't break yours, Sierra. And I told your brother as much today, as well, when I talked to him. But now I'm telling you."

There's something else I need to tell him too, though. "I was worried about relationships and time and balancing it all, but I already love dating you because it's not hard to make time for you. Like we talked about on the flight to Hawaii—it's quality, not quantity. I truly believe that," I say. "And everything is quality with you."

"Everything is the best with us."

His eyes flood with emotions—the same ones I feel, I suspect, as he grabs my hand and tugs me close, my breasts flush with his chest. My fiancé sighs happily then runs his fingers through my hair. "Missed you," he murmurs, then dusts his lips over mine.

"Missed you too," I whisper against his lips, as my cat rubs against my leg.

I laugh, separating. "Tom is in a lovey mood today," I say, my gaze sailing to my black and white beast.

"It's going around." Chance bends down to scratch Tom's chin, and I fall a little more for the man.

When Chance stands, he wiggles a brow, then scoops me into his arms. "And now I'd like to make love to my fiancée," he says.

Heat flares through me. "So impulsive of you."

In a minute, we're in my room, stripped down to nothing, and the man I'm engaged—*engaged!*—to puts on a condom and slides into me. I gasp, pleasure flowing through every cell.

"Mmm. You feel incredible," he murmurs as he sinks in all the way, filling me to the hilt. I lift my knees toward my chest, giving him permission to take me the way I want him to.

The way he wants to.

"Have me," I urge.

And he does, fucking me hard and deep, with so much passion that I'm racing toward the edge in mere minutes, bliss and lust twisting beautifully inside me.

He's rough at the same time that he's tender, and it's everything I ever wanted sex to be and so much more.

It's with the man I love.

Who also happens to be my husband, and now, my fiancé.

Life can be funny like that, if you just give in to happiness.

* * *

Later, as we curl up under the covers, Tom tucks his paws under his chest, a serene look on his furry face.

EPILOGUE

Chance

A little later

TJ rakes his gaze over my attire, studying me with intense eyes.

"What? You picked the suit. You damn well better like it," I say, trying to figure out what's wrong.

He shakes his head. "It's so easy to wind you up. Just one look and you're worried."

I roll my eyes. "It is my wedding day."

He pats my shoulder. "I know. I shouldn't enjoy messing with you so much, yet I do."

"I can't wait to mess with you on your wedding day."

A cough bursts from him. "You're killing me."

"Like that's so implausible?" I ask.

"It's a little implausible, me getting hitched. Love is

not in the cards for this guy. Anyway, you look good," he says, then pulls me in for a hug. "I'm happy for you, Chance."

I smile into the embrace. "Me too. Thanks for being here for me. For everything."

When we separate, he nods solemnly. "Always."

We leave my place—soon to be mine and Sierra's—and head to The Spotted Zebra.

As soon as we step inside, I spot my beautiful, brilliant bride. She's perched on a bar stool, decked out in a simple white wedding dress that hits her knees. Nothing fancy, just those spaghetti straps and, I bet, white lace underneath.

Oh yes.

I can't wait to undress my wife on our wedding night.

A second time around.

The bar opens in thirty minutes on a mid-January Saturday night. Zoey and the new bartender from Vegas will be serving—both the regular patrons and the private party of the Blackwood-Ashford wedding.

It's a small affair. Just close friends and close family.

But that's what matters.

I make my way to the woman I've dated for the last couple months. We've gone out to dinner, played pool, sang karaoke, and we've stayed in watching British comedies, watering plants, and arranging flowers.

I've also ripped off countless pairs of panties and dismantled plenty of bras.

And replaced them.

My fiancée-wife has an overstuffed lingerie drawer, and that makes the both of us happy.

But what makes me happier is heading into the game room, where an officiant waits for us.

Everyone gathers around—Grant and Declan, Crosby and Nadia, Holden and Reese, Clementine and Skyler, Trish and Blake, TJ, Frankie, Erin, Harlan and his little daughter Abby, as well as Sierra's grandparents and my own parents.

The officiant begins, and soon, she's asking, "And do you, Chance Ashford, take this woman to be your wife, to love and cherish for the rest of your days?"

Easiest answer ever. "I do," I say, looking into Sierra's eyes and feeling certainty and love.

"And do you, Sierra Blackwood, take this man to be your husband, to love and cherish for the rest of your days?"

My fiancée grins at me, her eyes already shining with tears. "I do."

"You may kiss the bride."

I kiss my bride for the second time around.

It's a wedding do-over—a replay of sorts.

Yet it feels new and completely meant to be as my wife who became my fiancée becomes my wife once again.

We separate, grinning like the happily married fools we are, then enjoy chocolate-covered strawberries and cake with our close friends and family.

Later that night, we don our *Just Married* sashes that I saved from Vegas. They are one helluva souvenir of the first wedding to my incredible wife.

I take a picture of my bride and me and post it.

Just married to the love of my life!

That about sums it up.

When we return to her place that night, we find a note under the door from her neighbor.

The cat sitter.

EPILOGUE

Tom

A cat love story

Ah, humans.

The dilemmas they faced.

Like, moving.

Tom suspected they'd be relocating any day. The boxes gave it away. There were boxes everywhere in his home.

He surmised all that talking was over moving.

Perhaps they'd even discussed how the cat would handle moving across town.

Please.

People.

The cat could handle it fine.

Cats could handle anything.

Humans invested every little decision with such monumentality. And there was always so much talking, as if that were the solution to anything, when actually, that was rarely the case.

Typical of the lesser species.

Cats had already evolved well beyond humans. They could speak in a more beautiful tongue. They could communicate everything in hisses, meows, and well-placed purrs.

After all, the great gift of purring had made all the difference for Tom a few months ago when he'd discovered a certain someone. Just the thought of the Siamese next door made him kick up his motor.

She revved his engine, all right.

Lady Cat.

Talk about a sexy feline.

She had it going on with that tail—lush, long, and fluffy.

The second he'd spotted that majestic tail, one afternoon while his mistress was gone, his kitty heart beat faster.

Raced harder.

Tom had been snoozing in the sun on the windowsill—naturally—when she'd walked by across the garden rooftop.

The sight of such a lovely lady had rousted him from his seventh nap of the day.

He'd slinked under the half-open window to outside, eager to make her furry acquaintance.

Meow . . .

It was love at first tail.

She'd twined hers around his, and their purr boxes went wild.

He fell for her paw over collar.

Little did his person know what he'd been up to during the days and, truth be told, the nights.

When the woman departed for that thing she called work, leaving Tom with those sweet little orders to be good, to behave, he'd done the opposite.

He'd been a very bad boy.

Sauntering out the open window.

Sidling up to Lady Cat.

Getting to know the lovely Siamese better and better each afternoon and evening. They'd napped together.

Oh, dear God, those naps.

Afternoons in the sun followed by evenings under the stars.

They could sleep all day, it seemed.

Probably all night too.

Sometimes his person asked why he was so happy.

He'd tried to tell her that day when she was distraught. The day he'd rubbed relentlessly, pushing his body against her leg, purring louder than he'd ever purred before.

Love was the answer.

He'd found it in Lady Cat.

He'd wanted his person to find it too.

And she had, it seemed, in the big, tall man.

But now, if they moved, what would happen to the beauty Tom enjoyed all those rooftop trysts with?

Admittedly, the cat was worried.

Worry was unfamiliar to him.

Cats didn't worry, except about where the next slices of tuna might come from.

But he was anxious too about that note that had arrived by a secret doorway whoosh a few hours ago when the woman was gone.

What did it say?

Was it an invitation from Lady Cat to slip away somewhere?

Later that night, the woman and the man stumbled into the home, giggling, whispering sweet nothings.

"Oh," the woman said, stopping to pick up the note. "It's from Lynn."

The man beamed. "Is it what I think it is?"

"I hope so," the woman said, opening the note then clutching her heart. "She's ours, Chance. She's ours."

The man raised a hand in the air, victorious. "Yes!"

"The shelter approved our application to adopt Lady Cat."

Meow?

What were they saying? What was the news?

The woman bent down, scratched his chin, stroked his head. "You want to come live with Chance and me and Lady Cat at his place?"

Please, let it be good news. He couldn't bear to part with Lady Cat.

Perhaps there was a way for Tom and his love to have a few more hours together. He could only hope.

Later that night, he jumped onto the humans' bed and purred, doing his best to tell them his wishes—*bring the Siamese.*

Please, oh kitty please.

Everything was easier if you purred more.

Didn't they understand? If they were cats, they certainly would.

He spent the rest of the night pacing. He couldn't even enjoy the boxes properly. Couldn't even jump into them, let alone out again.

What would happen to his Lady Cat?

But in the morning, he heard the pretty meow he'd come to love.

"She's here," the woman called out. Tom opened one eye, perked up an ear, and leapt out of bed.

He'd fallen asleep after all. It happened to cats.

But now, he was wide awake and ready.

He stretched his lithe body, lifted his lush tail, and sashayed to the front door where the woman held—be still, his beating heart—the love of his furry life.

Roar!

Lady Cat was here.

The woman set her down, and it was love at first tail all over again.

Much like it had been for the humans.

* * *

A few days later, they moved into the man's place where he puttered around talking to plants and cooking meals for his woman, and the two of them curled up together on the couch to watch comedies where they talked in funny voices.

Then they curled up together on the bed to do other things.

Tom understood. Sometimes a man just wanted to snuggle up with his woman.

Tom did just that, cuddling with Lady Cat, as the man and the woman laughed, and sighed, and kissed.

And lived happily ever after.

THE END

Curious about TJ? The twin who's taking a break from romance? His life is about to change when he has to fake a romance with an ex-hookup to finish his novel! Can he pull off a pretend relationship with the cocky, charming movie star he regrets? Find out in HOPELESSLY BROMANTIC! A preview follows.

Interested in Harlan's romance? Be sure to order THE BOYFRIEND PLAYBOOK! You won't believe what goes down when Harlan runs into a jilted bride from his past! You'll find a preview below!

And Shane's and Clementine's romance comes in THE VIRGIN SCORECARD, a collection of sexy novellas.

Be sure to sign up for my mailing list to be the first to know when swoony, sexy new romances are available or on sale!

. . .

Chapter One of Hopelessly Romantic

TJ

Things that suck—when your ex-boyfriend dates your . . . ex-boyfriend.

Things that don't suck—when you finally find the inspiration you've been scouring the city for.

There. Right there.

The second I run into Flynn and Caine holding hands as they order tacos at a food truck in Central Park on a Sunday afternoon while I finish my jog, my first thought isn't the obvious *they're talking about me*.

Not even when Flynn spots me, lifts a hand in a perfunctory wave, then when Caine follows his lead, waving too.

Nope.

My first and most epic thought is—*They're talking about me and that would be such a brilliant idea for a book, like, say, maybe the one that's massively overdue to my publisher*.

See you later, exes.

I don't end my run after all. I fly home on fleet feet to Chelsea, bound up four flights of stairs, flip open my laptop, and crack my knuckles.

It is on.

This guy has a book idea at long last.

After all these months of blank pages, words are flowing through my veins.

I write and I write and I write.

Goodbye, trashcan full of proverbial crumpled up pieces of paper.

Hello, brilliant idea for my next novel.

After a whole lot of nothing in the creativity department for several long, painful, idea-free months—and months vacant of ideas are almost as bad as sexless months, a drought I also know far too well—this surely is my breakthrough.

At last.

A few days and countless cups of coffee later, I've got almost ten chapters.

I've ordered in most meals and forgotten others, too, because that's how it works when the muse strikes. You don't stop to snack on Swedish fish or shove salted-caramel pretzels in your mouth. You just *do*.

You serve the gods of inspiration. And have I ever served.

I'm like that crazed author in a movie, tapping madly away, the *clack-clack-clack* of keys the soundtrack in my apartment till I yank the pages from the typewriter and slap them down on my agent's desk.

Okay, obviously I don't write on a typewriter. I'm not a Luddite. Also that's super wasteful when it comes paper.

But after a quick re-read on ye olde laptop, I send this bad boy to my agent.

Five minutes later, he replies with a hallelujah then tells me to swing by in an hour since he'll have it read by then.

I pump a fist, then push away from the couch to take a shower. Even when inspiration strikes, I'd never leave the house smelling like, well, like people think writers smell.

My goal in life is to smell like a magazine ad looks, and I accomplish that in fifteen minutes, then get dressed quickly, tugging on jeans and grabbing a short-sleeve button-down I snagged at a thrift shop. Bonus that it shows off my arms. Double bonus? The cute illustrations of foxes that cover the fabric.

Looking hip, I head uptown on a late spring morning in Manhattan. I push through the revolving glass door of Nathan's building, eager for his feedback.

It's gonna be good.

Bring it on. The *welcome back, TJ*. The *we know you're late on your deadline, but we love you so fucking much. And you're brilliant and incredible, and you're clearly already penning a fantastic follow-up, so go write more.*

A minute later, I exit the elevator on the eleventh floor. From behind the reception desk, Zoe waves excitedly at me, her chunky bracelets jingling and jangling against themselves, revealing bits and pieces of the tattoos of vines that line her arms. "TJ, I wrote five thousand words last night," she says, wildfire in her eyes. "You've inspired me."

See?

Everything is new again.

Everyone is creating.

"It's in the air, Zoe." I hold up a hand to high five. "Keep it up."

"I will. Also, Nathan said to just wave you in."

How about that? I don't even have to wait to see the

dude. I knew it. He loves the premise of my new book too.

But when I reach his corner suite, he's still seated at his desk.

Staring at the screen.

Scratching his head.

Weird.

I expected him to be standing in the doorway, blowing on a trumpet, hailing my return.

Parking my hands on my hips, I clear my throat. "Hello? Where is the parade? The ticker tape? The marching band? I'll wait for them but, man, I normally expect you to be a little faster."

Nathan lifts his gaze from his screen.

His face is completely inscrutable, his dark eyes behind his black glasses a total closed book.

But I'm undeterred.

I won't let a little thing like an agent's unreadable face get me down, though I kinda wish Nathan would say something. I do like praise. It's oxygen.

I wag a finger at him. "Wait. I know what you did. You got me a singing telegram, didn't you? One of those *Magic Mike* strippers is going to jump out in just a second and tell me how awesome you thought the pages were." I cross my arms. "I'll wait."

With a beleaguered sigh, Nathan takes off his glasses, sets them down on his desk, and scrubs a hand along the back of his neck. "For the record, if I ever order you a stripper, it'll be a cop."

"Sweet. I ordered one the other night after a burger and a beer. It was basically a perfect night," I deadpan.

A small smile lifts the corners of his mouth. "*That.*" Nathan stabs his finger against the computer screen. "Why isn't *that* in *this*?"

My brow furrows, and I step into his office, head to the cushy blue chair across from his desk, and park myself in it. "Why isn't what in what?"

"That kind of humor. That kind of wit. Stripper jokes. Humor. Badinage. Wit. Banter."

My face goes blank.

At least, I think it does. I can't see my face obviously.

But it feels blank from the shock of his comment. I flap my hand in the direction of his computer. "That's all in there. That's really fucking funny. And full of heart. How could you not see it?"

"Is it?" Nathan clears his throat and reads from the screen. *"Ten Rules for Dating My Ex. Chapter One. Tanner. The first rule of dating? Don't go out with a dude with a one-syllable name. I learned that the hard way the other day."*

"That's a good rule. See? *Flynn. Caine.*" I drag both out like their names are a warning. "If only I had known that before I got involved."

"Allow me to read more."

"Please do." With a smile, I kick back in the chair, happiness washing over me. I've always loved when people read to me. There's little I love more than being told a good tale.

Well, pizza and sex. I like them both better.

Not in that order though.

I listen contentedly as the hero sets up his dilemma —*Lessons learned from the front lines of dating, since it's a battlefield out there.*

When Nathan trails off at the end of the second page, I scoot forward in the chair.

Doesn't he like it?

Oh shit. Does he . . . hate it? Are my words complete and utter garbage?

"TJ," he says heavily, and, uh-oh, that sounds less like a seal of approval and more like a veto.

Worry wiggles down my spine. "Yes?"

"There's no romance in here. This is a breakup book."

I bristle. Like I've never bristled before. He's wrong. He's just wrong. "Did you read all ten chapters? It's a set-up for a romance. He's just . . . well, Tanner is just . . ." I cast about for words to describe my hero's situation. "He's recapping the lessons learned from past breakups. Licking his wounds and all."

Nathan stares at me like his eyes are a bullshit detector. "Yes, I get that. Loud and clear. But where's the romance?"

It's . . .

It's in . . .

Isn't it in there?

My mind flips back to the pages I wrote. "I'm sure it's there. It has to be. I meant it to be."

He shakes his head, his expression rueful. "The first ten chapters are about his breakup. There's zero romance. Zero dates. Zero set-up. I don't even know what the trope or the plot is. Is it enemies to lovers? Friends to lovers?"

I cringe at the last one. Whip my head back and

forth. No way would I write friends to lovers—not after what went down with Flynn.

"Opposites attract? Forbidden romance? Fake romance."

My stomach churns.

Dammit.

I slump down in the chair, drop my forehead into my hand. There isn't a shred of romance in *Rules for Dating My Ex*. Shoulders sagging, I drag a hand through my hair. "I don't know what the hell to do, Nathan," I say, confessing what I think he already suspects. "Everyone's expecting this epic love story like *Top-Notch Boyfriend*. That was easy to write. I was . . ."

But I can't finish the sentence.

I've written books before Flynn.

Hell, I wrote nine.

But none that big, that powerful, that swoony as the 'epic guy meets guy and falls head over oxfords in love' story that was *Top-Notch Boyfriend*.

The romance that vaulted me from midlist to bestseller.

That made my apartment possible, my life possible, my freedom from worries possible.

But only if I can pull off another.

Nathan's intensity vanishes. In its place is concern. "Yes, you were in love, TJ. It drove you to write. To feel. To dig deep into your soul for your art. But it didn't last and that sucks. I get it. I've been there before."

I turn away, peering out the window of his Amsterdam Avenue offices, staring at the city below. Millions of people in this naked city. Some days, it feels as if everybody here knows what happened. The guy who inspired the story that topped bestseller lists and made me a mint dumped me publicly, painfully, and with disastrous consequences for my career.

I jerk my gaze back to Nathan. "Fine. I'll try again. Another approach. I'll—"

"—You'll introduce the trope in Chapter One," he says, laying it out there, crisp and business-like. "You'll bring the other hero on page in chapter two. And how about a kiss by chapter eight?"

My jaw drops. "You have the whole thing plotted out, man?"

His grin makes it clear this isn't his first time at the rodeo. "I know a thing or two about what makes for a good book. I've also read all yours. That's what works—that kind of strategy. Make *this one* work."

My agent pulls no punches. With intense eyes, he delivers the final verdict, pointing to the screen. "This *anti-romance* isn't what anybody actually wants to read in your romance novel, *King TJ.*"

It's like a shot to the heart, especially when he uses the name my readers have given me. Lovingly given me. But lately, they've all been knocking on my social media doors, asking for the next book that's been delayed, and then delayed some more.

Soon, if I don't deliver, they'll move on to the next writer.

Someone who actually puts out more books.

And it hurts so much because . . . that excitement I felt while writing was classic brain trickery. My mind fooled me into thinking this story was good. My fingers were flying, so I figured I was spinning solid gold.

When I was spinning solid gold shit.

I drag my hands through my hair, heaving out a sigh of admission. "What do I do?"

"You've written ten books. All with great reviews. One of them was a massive, huge, fireball of a hit, that turned your backlist into money trees — incidentally that's my favorite kind of tree. So, can't you just do that again? Write another good love story?"

His question is a reasonable one. I *should* be able to. There's no logical reason why I can't pull it off. "Absolutely. I just need to focus on what they all had in common. The magic ingredient."

Nathan's eyes say *you've gotta be kidding me*. "Could it be . . . oh, I don't know, you believed in romance back then? You were fucking romantic. You went on dates. With Caine, with Flynn, with Dante, with Gabriel."

"Feel free to just list all my exes. The reminders are great for my confidence," I say drily.

He pays me no mind. "And you took them to baseball games, or to play pinball, or to go thrifting or do game nights. You felt the mojo. You were getting out there." He gestures to my arms. "From the looks of it, the only place you're going these days is to the gym."

My eyes stray to my biceps. The guns are bigger than they were a year ago. But nothing wrong that that. Lots of dudes like fit guys. "Gym equipment doesn't break your heart."

"But rock star writers who don't deliver their next novel break mine," Nathan says, clutching at his chest.

"You don't want to do that, do you? Or, say, break your contract?"

"You know what the alpha lawyer hero in *The Size Principle* said—*Contracts are made to be broken*," I say, offering a lopsided grin, like that'll cover up the case of my missing inspiration. "Maybe my next hero should be a detective, a cool-as-a-cucumber private eye, who'll track down my muse."

"Art imitates life, so if that's what it takes . . ." Nathan stands, strides around his desk, looking all sharp in his slacks and his tailored shirt, setting a hand on my shoulder. "Listen, you've got a contract and a deadline. There are only so many ways I can do a song and dance for Brooks & Bailey," he says, gentle this time.

"Yes, I know my publisher has given me three extensions already," I say plainly, still embarrassed that he had to ask for them.

"This isn't like you. You popped out books like you were making kettle corn at the farmer's market back when you were the swinging stud of New York. When you were dating all over town. How hard can it be to start dating again? Especially with those arms," he says with a wink.

"Romance and me are on a timeout," I mutter, admitting the sad, stark truth.

He cups his ear. "What's that? Oh, that's the sound of the buzzer on your timeout. It's time to get back in the game, TJ. Get on a dating app. We don't even have to use Grindr anymore. We can do Tinder. We can do anything. Hell, you can do Boyfriend Material and level all the way up," he says, and I cringe. "Is that such a bad idea?"

"Do you have any idea what would happen if TJ Hardman was available for any reader or listener to bang? I'd be the talk of social media. Of every gay romance reader group. No way. I can't just put myself out there on an app."

Nathan smiles, the nefarious grin that only a true shark of a literary agent can pull out. The man gestures grandly to himself. "Then I shall be your app. Be ready this Friday at eight o'clock for a date at the St. James Theater, home of the Sweeney Todd revival."

Is he for real? I eye him suspiciously because, of course, that is a very suspicious statement. "You're married to a Tony-winning actor. The lead in that show. I'm not going out with you to see your husband."

"Happily married, I might add, and Tremaine is fabulous in Sondheim. But I also work at a talent agency that reps writers, directors and actors. That means, King TJ, you can just think of *me* as your dating app, since we've got someone for you."

Shark? He's more like a bionic shark descended from Neptune himself and crossbred with a fire-breathing dragon of the sea. "*We've?* Who the hell is we?"

He taps his chest. "Raphael and moi."

"Raphael, the agent down the hall who reps actors and movie stars?"

He points at me like I've won a prize on a game show. "Give this man a cookie!"

I groan. "What are you and Raphael cooking up?"

The wicked glee spreads to Nathan's irises. "Does the name Jude Fox ring a bell?"

It rings all the bells. Namely, the chimes from eight years ago when I met Jude in London.

But why the hell is Nathan is bringing up Jude? "Yes, I saw *If Found Please Return* at the arthouse cinema a couple months ago," I say, since I don't need to let on I've seen Jude up close and personal too.

"He was fantastic in that flick. And he's been nommed for an award." Nathan grins diabolically. He might as well twirl a handlebar mustache.

"All right. No more monologuing like a villain revealing how he did it. Just gimme the deets," I say.

Nathan points at me. "You need some inspiration in the form of dating, and guess what? Jude needs something too."

Yup. Called it. Bionic Shark with Evil Genius Brain. "Let me guess. He needs a . . ." I make a rolling gesture with my hand as I wait for Nathan to finish the connect-the-dots game he's playing.

"Jude needs a very appropriate fake boyfriend. And his agent and I have chosen you."

Wait a hot second. I take umbrage at one thing. "How the hell am I appropriate? That doesn't sound like a compliment."

"It is, TJ. You're America's Sweet and Hot Romance Writer. You're the perfect antidote to his last beau. And listen, the way I see things is you can either keep *not* writing your book, or you can go on some dates and find some inspiration again, and write the book that everyone's waiting for you to pen." He takes a deep inhale, sounding wholly satisfied. "Which option sounds more appealing? Door number one or door number two?"

That's an excellent question.

But I'm choosing door number three. "Getting my balls waxed by a first-timer at a shady clinic with one-star reviews," I say.

Nathan doesn't blink. "And I imagine that's how Brooks & Bailey feels every time you don't deliver your book." He gestures to his phone, waving airily at it. "If you have a better suggestion, I'm all ears. If not, let me know what I should tell Raphael."

That Jude should have shown up for our date eight years ago.

That he's only gotten better-looking over the years.

That I have no interest in fake dating a former fling.

And yet . . . the clock doesn't stop ticking on my deadline.

I meet Nathan's stare head on. "Friday at eight works for me. I'll meet him at the St. James Theater."

Nathan grins, returns to his desk, and sits down. "Great. And I think you'll find it more enjoyable than scrotal depilation. But hey, that's ultimately for you to decide. And since we should probably hash out some of the details before you make your dating debut, I've conveniently arranged a little coffee date for you in thirty minutes time."

Sharks have nothing on my agent.

. . .

Find out what happens next in HOPELESSLY BROMANTIC!

Interested in Harlan's romance? You won't believe what goes down when the football star runs into a jilted bride from his past! Here's a preview of THE BOYFRIEND PLAYBOOK...

For the next few hours, I have a blast throwing strikes and gutter-balls alike with my friends until, one by one, they peel off. As the clock ticks closer to ten, it's just Cooper—my quarterback—and me, and we chat as we make our way out, passing the bar inside the bowling alley where my gaze catches on a woman in a formal white dress.

That's odd enough to rate a look, but something about her feels achingly familiar.

Possibilities nag at me all the way to the exit then won't let me leave.

At the door, I tell Cooper I'll see him at training camp. "I swore I saw someone who looked familiar. I'll catch you later. I need to go check on something."

He lifts his chin in a goodbye. "See you at camp."

I turn around, the blonde profile triggering a memory that tugs me back to the bar.

Could it be?

Is that . . . her?

A tingle of excitement coasts over my skin at the mere possibility.

When I reach the bar, I take a deep breath and look in, then I shake my head in amazement.

The woman in white is none other than someone who, seven years ago, I desperately wanted to see again.

And she's wearing a wedding dress as she orders another shot of tequila.

Grab THE BOYFRIEND PLAYBOOK!

ALSO BY LAUREN BLAKELY

FULL PACKAGE, the #1 New York Times Bestselling romantic comedy!

BIG ROCK, the hit New York Times Bestselling standalone romantic comedy!

THE SEXY ONE, a New York Times Bestselling standalone romance!

THE KNOCKED UP PLAN, a multi-week USA Today and Amazon Charts Bestselling standalone romance!

MOST VALUABLE PLAYBOY, a sexy multi-week USA Today Bestselling sports romance! And its companion sports romance, MOST LIKELY TO SCORE!

WANDERLUST, a USA Today Bestselling contemporary romance!

COME AS YOU ARE, a Wall Street Journal and multi-week USA Today Bestselling contemporary romance!

PART-TIME LOVER, a multi-week USA Today Bestselling contemporary romance!

UNBREAK MY HEART, an emotional second chance USA Today Bestselling contemporary romance!

BEST LAID PLANS, a sexy friends-to-lovers USA Today Bestselling romance!

The Heartbreakers! The USA Today and WSJ Bestselling rock star series of standalone!

P.S. IT'S ALWAYS BEEN YOU, a sweeping, second chance romance!

MY ONE WEEK HUSBAND, a sexy standalone romance!

CONTACT

I love hearing from readers! You can find me on Twitter at LaurenBlakely3, Instagram at LaurenBlakelyBooks, Facebook at LaurenBlakelyBooks, or online at LaurenBlakely.com. You can also email me at laurenblakelybooks@gmail.com

Printed in Great Britain
by Amazon

67121368R00169